The
Steps

The Steps

Rachel Cohn

Aladdin Paperbacks
New York London Toronto Sydney

First Aladdin Paperbacks edition September 2004

ALADDIN PAPERBACKS
An imprint of Simon & Schuster
Children's Publishing Division
1230 Avenue of the Americas
New York, NY 10020

Also available in a Simon & Schuster Books for Young Readers hardcover edition.
Designed by Russell Gordon
The text of this book was set in Aldine 721.

Printed in the United States of America
2 4 6 8 10 9 7 5 3 1

The Library of Congress has cataloged the hardcover edition as follows:
Cohn, Rachel.
The Steps / Rachel Cohn.—1st ed.
p. cm.
Summary: Over Christmas vacation, Annabel goes from her home in Manhattan to visit her father, his new wife, and her half and stepsiblings in Sydney, Australia.
ISBN 0-689-84549-9 (hc.)
[1. Stepfamilies—Fiction. 2. Family life—Fiction. 3. Australia—Fiction.] I. Title
PZ7.C6665 St 2003
[Fic]—dc21 2001057566
ISBN 0-689-87721-8 (pbk.)

For Anna and Martha

℃℥

Thanks to David Gale, Steve Geck, Ellia Bisker, and extra thanks to the real Jack, Nell, Ben, Lucy, and Annabel in Melbourne, with love from Rita.

Chapter 1

If you think it's hard keeping track of all the Steps in my life, try being me.

The Steps are the bazillion stepbrothers, stepsisters, and half siblings my parents keep laying on me. Follow this.

First, there are Angelina and Jack, my parents. I've called my parents by their first names for as long as I can remember. Maybe if they were normal parents who stayed together (or even bothered to get married), or maybe if they had regular day jobs, I would call them Mom and Dad, but that would be, like, so *Brady Bunch*, and we are so not Brady. Besides, Angelina and Jack were the ones who taught me to call them by their first names. Angelina said Mom was "too uptight a word" for her to hear, and Jack said being called Dad made him feel like an "old coot."

Angelina's an actress and Jack was a comedian.

They met when they were both waiters at a hip restaurant in Manhattan. They were "young, dumb, 'n' in love," according to Bubbe, my grandma. They moved in together and had me. I'm Annabel Whoopi Schubert and I'm twelve years old, but I'm "going on thirteen with a vengeance," as Bubbe says.

After Angelina and Jack finished being "young, dumb, 'n' in love," they became yelling and fighting adult folks. After a couple really bad years being miserable all the time, they split up when I was nine.

Then Jack met Penny and moved to Australia to be with her. Penny has a daughter, Lucy, who is the same age as me, and a son, Angus, who's in kindergarten. They call it "kindie" in Australia. Jack thinks it's clever that those people in Australia are always cutting off words and adding *ie* to them, like *noodies* for *noodles* and *brekkie* for *breakfast*. I don't think it's clever. I think it's lazy. My baby half sister, Beatrice, who is the daughter of Jack and Penny and also the half sister of Lucy and Angus, will end up talking like that one day. Imagine that, my own blood sister, and she's going to speak with an Australian accent and cut off her words and end them in *ie*. Please.

Back to Angelina, my mom, who got way too into her role as PTA treasurer and started dating the president of the PTA, Harvey Weideman. Harvey is the divorced father of Wheaties, only the dorkiest kid in the whole seventh grade. I don't even remember Wheaties' real name. That's what we call him at our school, the Progress School on the Upper West Side. Wheaties is short and scrawny and goes around singing folk songs. He's the last boy you'd ever see on a cereal box. Now Angelina's pregnant, and she and Harvey are getting married, so I'm going to have another half sibling and another step. I wonder if I will be the first girl in the world with a stepbrother called Wheaties.

The other step is Lucy and Angus's former stepbrother, Ben. He's not my step technically, so I think it's okay that I kissed him once.

But I'm getting ahead of myself. Let me take you back to Christmas break.

It all started because Lucy stole my dad.

Chapter 2

I didn't want to go to Sydney, Australia. I wanted to spend Christmas break in Manhattan with my best friend Justine. We had planned to go ice-skating at Rockefeller Center every day and shopping at the after-Christmas sale at Bloomingdale's. We were going to make prank phone calls to Wheaties and his geek friends and try on makeup at Sephora and then go scream with the *TRL* crowd at MTV in Times Square.

Then Justine bailed. Her parents decided to go skiing for the holidays. Wheaties stopped answering his phone. Angelina decided she was "so over" Jack moving to Australia and it was time for me to go see my dad. Angelina was going to some luau paradise in Hawaii with Wheaties' dad. Even Bubbe bailed on me. She went to Florida.

I had been so excited about hanging with Justine over the vacay that I hadn't considered going to see

Jack or my new half sister, Beatrice. I didn't especially care about meeting the Steps for the first time. I wanted to stay home in New York City, the greatest city in all the world.

Well, I guess I really did want to see Jack, and I kinda wanted to see Beatrice because I wondered if my actual blood sister looked like me, but I totally, absolutely, completely did not want to go all the way to the Steps' turf in Australia. But I was stuck.

That whole plane ride to Australia I couldn't even watch the movies. I was too busy remembering what Lucy had done.

Jack was still living with us when I was nine, but he and Angelina fought all the time. One night Jack didn't come home at all after a late-night comedy gig. Angelina thought I was sleeping and didn't know, but I was awake and I heard her crying into the phone all night. When he finally came home early in the morning, I could hear him telling her over and over, nothing happened. Whatever didn't happen, Jack and Angelina were never right again. He moved out a month later. Soon after that Angelina and I moved into Bubbe's massive apartment, which overlooks Central Park on the Upper West Side of Manhattan.

It was kind of cool for a while. Even though he lived in Brooklyn, I actually saw more of Jack once he and Angelina split. Probably because he and Angelina weren't always tired from constant fighting. He met me every day after school, and sometimes we'd go in-line skating in Central Park and other times we'd hang out at a coffee shop, talking and reading until dinnertime, and he coached my soccer team, and every Saturday we went to a movie together.

Then one Saturday he told me about this woman who had changed his life. Her name was Penny, and he'd met her when she was visiting from Australia. He loved her. He wanted to start a new life with her. He told me Penny had this ultimate, fantastic incredi-daughter named Lucy, who was just like me, and he knew I would love Lucy to death. He was moving to Australia to be with Penny and Lucy and Penny's son, Angus.

That's when things got bad.

Maybe he said he was moving to Australia to marry Penny, but part of me suspected he was moving to Australia to be with Lucy, too. Like she was a better daughter than me. Why else would a dad move ten thousand miles away to be with a new family?

The day Jack told me about his new family, he said, "Do I have your blessing?" I nodded and said yes because he's such a nice dad with the cutest face you ever saw and he looked so happy, but I crossed my fingers behind his back when I hugged him and really I was thinking no. Really I was thinking, *Lucy can borrow you until I figure out how to win you back.*

Things were really hard after Jack left. I cried alone in my room almost every night when Bubbe and Angelina thought I was sleeping. In my dreams I saw

Jack wearing a Crocodile Dundee hat, holding the Steps' hands, with a koala bear hanging from his shoulders, and the Steps singing, "He's ours now, he's ours now, na-na-na-na-na." Not even the fact that Jack called me every week and sent letters and little presents from Australia could fill the huge black hole in my heart created by his leaving. Eventually I got used to missing him and I stopped crying alone at night, but I refused to talk to the Steps on the phone, and when Jack came to visit me a year later, before Beatrice was born, I pretended not to be interested when he tried to tell me about Sydney, Australia, and about Penny and the Steps.

But now I was stuck going to Australia for Christmas break. Bubbe and Angelina wanted me to go. Jack had sent me E-mail every day for weeks before my trip, telling me what clothes to pack and describing all the things he wanted us to do together, with the Steps.

While the plane taking me to meet the Steps floated over gray clouds and endless ocean for what seemed like forever, I stared at the pictures of Lucy and Angus and plotted the ways I was going to aggravate them so much that they would become such terrible children that Jack would return home to New York City with me, where he belonged. It was true, what Jack had said—Lucy did look a little like me. She had light blond hair, only mine was longer and curlier and she had bangs and I didn't, and she had blue eyes and rosy cheeks and braces. Her braces were multicolored, which made her mouth look like a lollipop, I thought. I'm a traditionalist (that's what Bubbe says about me, because I like to watch old movies with her and look at all her old clothes from the '50s), so my braces are solid silver. I think multicolored lollipop-looking braces are too flashy, and I should know. One day I'm going to be a famous fashion designer.

Just looking at her pictures, I knew that Lucy was a fashion no-no. Angus, I could see from his pictures, was also hopeless. He had a mop of wild, curly blond hair and thick glasses, and—get this—in his picture he was wearing neon-colored striped pants with a paisley-print T-shirt that had a picture of a fish on it! I knew my first order of business when I got to Australia would be to speak with Penny about properly dressing Angus. I know what happens on the playground to kids who dress badly, because I have been torturing Wheaties about his fashion sense since nursery school.

I admit, all the time on the plane that I was thinking of ways to torture Lucy and Angus—like Plan A, accidentally spitting my bubble gum into their hair and then trying to take it out but really getting it gooed thick and impossible throughout their head, or Plan B, teaching them to make Jack's favorite "Famous New York–Style Spaghetti" with a whole cup of salt and a whole jar of olives (Jack's most hated food)—I was also worried. Jack had been living with Penny, Lucy, and Angus for two years. Beatrice, our new baby half sister, was almost a year old. Jack had been back to America to visit me in the two years since he'd moved to Australia, but I had still never met them, and I knew that in those two years they would have developed a secret family language only they could understand.

Bubbe, Angelina, and I have our own special understandings, how we know one another's feelings and thoughts without having to say them. Like how Bubbe knows when I did bad on a math test by the way I hug her when she meets me after school and how she'll make me turn the television off later in the evening and go over fractions and equations while we bake cookies, or how Angelina knows when I have been crying secretly in my room from missing Jack and she'll cancel an audition to take me to a half-price Broadway show or to a baseball game, like Jack used to do before Penny, Lucy, and Angus took him away. Or how I know when Angelina is bummed because she didn't get an acting part and I will make her a cappuccino, turn on the stereo, and put on what I call the sad-lady music—all these really cool ladies from like a million years ago with names like Dinah, Billie, and Etta, who sing about love and loss and what a difference a day makes.

Then there's my Bubbe. I can tell she is thinking about my dead grandpa when it's raining and she goes and sits on her plush chair and stares out the windows looking onto Central Park for hours and hours. When I see her like that, sometimes I'll curl up on her lap and nestle my head on her shoulder, and she'll tell me stories about my dead grandpa, about how they met when they were both campaigning in the 1950s for some guy called Adlai Stevenson (Adlai!) who wanted to be president, about their first date riding a boat on the Hudson River, circling Manhattan, and how they drove to Maryland a week later to get married and never looked back. "Grandpa sure wanted to see you grow into a young lady," she'll say. Bubbe likes to hear the sad-lady music too.

Two years had passed without me there to crack the secret family code that would have developed among Jack, Penny, Lucy, Angus, and Beatrice. I wondered if Lucy had figured out that on cold nights Jack loved to drink real hot chocolate not made from a mix, or that when he performed a bad set and the audience never laughed, that afterward, to cheer up, he liked to eat peanut M&Ms and watch Nick at Nite shows like *The Odd Couple* and *Bewitched*, but never ever *I Love Lucy*.

How I was going to figure out their secret family language and still manage to steal Jack back, I really, truly did not know. That's right, I, Annabel Whoopi Schubert, middle-namesake of Whoopi Goldberg, seventh-grade class president at the Progress School on the Upper West Side, future fashion designer whose clothes will one day be featured in every important fashion mag in the whole wide world, did not know how to win my dad back.

Chapter 3

The first thing I noticed about the Steps was that they called Jack "Dad."

I had been on planes from New York to Sydney for practically twenty-four hours, and I was tired and totally disoriented by the time the plane landed in Sydney. Then I had to stand around and make small talk with my "chaperone"—the flight attendant who kept calling herself an "air hostess." What was up with that, anyway? Just because she was Australian, now she was an "air hostess" instead of a regular American flight attendant? While she stood with me in the passport and luggage lines, I imagined her twirling around in blue-sky space serving red cocktails with green olives. As we waited the air hostess jabbered on and on about how much I was going to love Sydney, Australia. A lot that air hostess knew.

By the time I made it out to the passenger meeting

area, all I wanted was to see Jack and for him to carry me home.

"There she is, Dad!" a voice screamed when I emerged from customs. *Dad?*

I identified the pointy finger attached to the rosy, blond face as the Lucy whose pictures I had been inspecting on the plane. The curly-headed boy who came up to Lucy's waist was jumping up and down too. "That's Annabel, that's Annabel!" It seemed like everyone at the airport was staring at me, and they were all smiling at us like, *Oh, how cute are they.* The flight attendant/air hostess was grinning, all wide eyed and white teeth, like, *Awww. Oy vey,* as Bubbe would say! I was so embarrassed, I wanted the Steps to shut up before I'd even met them. Their unwelcome enthusiasm was causing a very uncool scene. And I couldn't jump into Jack's arms, as I'd been waiting to do the whole plane ride. He had baby Beatrice attached to his chest in a Snugli.

"What's that scowl all about, Anna-the-Belle?" Jack asked when I made it to them. His voice seemed deeper than I remembered. Hearing it live and in person, not a zillion miles away by phone, sounded so good. One nice thing, even if he couldn't lift me into his arms (maybe I'm a little too big anyway), he was grinning from ear to ear, and he leaned down to kiss my face again and again and again. It's so nice when people are happy to see you.

Except when those people are the Steps.

I could barely kiss my dad before Lucy jumped over

and—you're not going to believe this—hugged me! I was like, *Hello, I don't even know you, why are you hugging me,* but I didn't say anything. I was kind of shocked.

"I have been counting the days until you came! I've always wanted a sister my own age!" she squealed. My shocked head was squeezed against hers in that unwelcome hug. I noticed even more airport people watching us, smiling all kindly, like we were in some soda commercial and a band was playing music and we would all start to dance around in the luggage carts, swigging 7UP like one big, happy family.

Not.

"Me, too!" Angus shrieked. He wrapped his arms around my thigh. I was wearing extra-chic designer jeans that Bubbe had given me for my birthday, and I was not happy to have a five-year-old slobbering on them.

The Steps spoke in the weirdest accent, like if you had a science experiment and mixed together a British Tinkerbell fairy with a chef from Louisiana, then the way the Australian Steps spoke would be the result.

"Some folks here have been very excited to see you, Anna-the-Belle," Jack said. "Her, too." Beatrice was sleeping against his chest, and she had the longest eyelashes you ever saw and puffy red cheeks and soft black hair like an angel. She did not look anything like me or Jack, and she did not smell like an angel.

"Dad, Beatrice needs a nappy change," Lucy said.

She tried to lock her hand in mine, but I shook her off.

Dad? See what I mean about a secret understanding developing between Jack and the Steps in the two years since he'd been gone, a language that did not include me? Jack had told me a long time ago that Lucy and Angus's real father, Lachlan, had died in a car accident one month before Angus was born. He said things were really bad for Penny, Lucy, and Angus for a long time after that, but now they were better, much better.

"A nappy?" I said.

"That's a diaper," Jack said. "In Australia diapers are called nappies." I latched on to his hand.

I was pretty annoyed about the Steps, but I couldn't help but giggle at their strange choice of words.

I was too tired to talk, really, but it didn't matter. The Steps blabbered on and on as we walked out to the car. Lucy wanted to take me to some place called Darling Harbor, and Angus wanted me to see the giant clown face at a place called Luna Park. On and on and on they jabbered. I thought, *You people talk faster than New Yorkers, and even I didn't think that was possible.*

Jack looked different. The Jack I remembered from New York seemed like he was always staring at the sky, wondering what to do next. The Australia Jack walking us to the car looked taller, broader, more confident. Like he had found his place in the world.

Without me.

Chapter 4

You would not believe how warm it was as we walked from the airport to the car. I knew it was December. Charlie Brown, Rudolph, and Kris Kringle had already proved that on my television the last few weeks in Manhattan. Yet as I stepped outside the airport, the day after Christmas, the weather was balmy and warm, almost tropical.

"The weather feels like July, Jack," I said, suspicious. I held on to his belt straps, not letting go of him even when he was trying to put Beatrice into the car seat.

"I told you, that's because in the Southern Hemisphere the seasons are the opposite of those in America. You didn't believe me when I wrote you about that, did you, Annabel?" I let out my first and only laugh of the day right then. Jack, besides Angelina and Bubbe, knows me better than anybody. He knew that I didn't think it was actually possible to be in a place that felt like summer when I could see Christmas lights twinkling everywhere, even if he had promised it to be so. I needed to experience it to believe it.

Tilted weather for the hemisphere tilt. I took off my down vest and believed. *Tilted country*, I thought.

They drive on the left side of the road in Australia. How weird is that! I was sitting in what in America would be the driver's side of the car, and when I looked out the window at the freeway on the way home from the airport, the oncoming stream of traffic was on the right side of my vision. I screamed! For a second I thought all those cars were driving on the wrong side of the road and we were about to hit them. My scream started a chain reaction.

Beatrice, Angus, and Lucy were riding in the backseat. After I screamed, Beatrice woke up from her little snooze and started howling herself. Then Angus started whining about all the noise Beatrice was making, which made Lucy yell at him to shut up.

For a second I felt at home, like I was riding in a cab in Manhattan, only instead of honking horns and screeching brakes and yelling drivers, it was screaming children. It was chaos. That was fine with me.

Only the thing was, Jack didn't seem annoyed by all the noise—and he used to hate cab rides in Manhattan more than anybody I've ever known, said they were wild and scary. No, Jack was smiling to himself, like he was thinking: *This is right, this is how it should be.*

The view from my window changed as we exited off the freeway, and I was distracted from the backseat noise. All these famous places I'd seen on TV, like the Sydney Opera House and the Sydney Harbour Bridge, were suddenly passing right in front of my window. I wondered how Lucy would feel if she ever got to see the Statue of Liberty or the Empire State Building. I doubted she was cool enough to ever visit Manhattan, though. I was sure of it.

I can't say I was any more impressed with Penny than I was with the Steps. When we arrived home, Penny was standing on the porch of their cottage. (Cottage! Who ever heard of living in a cottage when you're in the city? Cities are supposed to have apartment buildings, not little cottage houses.) Penny was biting her fingernails. I looked down at my own gold glitter-painted fingernails, which Angelina had painted before I left for Australia. Angelina never bit her nails.

As Jack helped Beatrice and the Steps out of the car I stayed seated, inspecting Penny from the car window. She was small but muscular, and she wore all black, so at least I could relate to her clothing. She had black hair cut really short, and she wore these—I hated to give her credit—most excellent black leather calf-length riding boots over her black leggings. She was pretty-okay, not pretty-beautiful like Angelina, but sort of spooky and attractive in a plain kind of way. As she walked toward the car she looked more nervous than I felt.

For a second I was scared. What if she hated me as much as I hated her and the Steps for taking Jack away? It had never occurred to me that she could possibly do anything other than adore me, since I had known Jack the longest and of course he loved me best. But when I saw her biting her nails and taking cautious steps toward me, I realized she was just as scared as I was. Maybe she was scared I would take Jack back home with me.

That thought gave me courage. *She should be scared,* I thought, to even the score. She and her Dad-calling children had taken away my Jack. I needed to remember that so I could not fall under the spell of her thrift-store-chic look.

"Welcome, Annabel," she said when I got out of the car. I looked down and scrunched my shoulders so she would not try to hug me. Her accent was soft and pretty; she didn't sound anything like Crocodile Dundee. "I've heard so many great things about you. We're so happy you're here." She pronounced "great" like "graayate."

I thought, *I see your bitten-down fingernails. I know you're not thrilled to have me here.* I mumbled, "Thanks," and to myself I thought, *I am not going to like you, but I have to admit those are killer boots you are wearing.*

Chapter 5

So I had barely been in Australia a few hours, and already I was teed off that Lucy and Angus were calling Jack "Dad" (I don't even call him that, and I'm his real daughter), that Penny wasn't ugly and horrible, and the fact that I was stranded halfway around the world from Manhattan, U.S. of A., when Jack made it worse that first night.

He prepared chicken cacciatore, my former favorite food, for dinner.

Obviously, Jack had forgotten the E-mail I sent him where I explained about the seventh-grade class elections at the Progress School, which had resulted in my becoming a vegetarian.

The seventh-grade class at the Progress School has twenty-three kids: ten girls and thirteen boys. Of those twenty-three, eight kids are vegetarian, two are totally vegan (Wheaties, of course, is one of those kids—I think he does it just to annoy his dad), three are strictly kosher, five are lactose intolerant, and one eats only macrobiotic foods. I know because I polled the class and created a very superior pie-chart graph showing our food habits for a social studies project.

In order for me to win that election as class president, I needed what Justine, who nominated me, called a "gimmick." My rival for the election was Brittany Carlson, whose father is, like, the most powerful lawyer in Manhattan. Bubbe used to say she wouldn't want to be on the wrong side of him if, God forbid, Angelina ever got a divorce—then Bubbe would mumble, "And God forbid my daughter should get married already in order to have a divorce." Brittany's dad—I'm so not kidding—funded her campaign with candy-filled plastic pumpkins that had Brittany's picture plastered all over them, which Brittany conveniently placed on our cafeteria tables!

Brittany is basically pukefying. She has big blue eyes and long, honey-colored hair, which she is constantly brushing with this fancy wood brush that has a holographic sticker of that Rachel girl from *Friends* on the handle. Aside from the unfortunate fact that she is a very pretty girl who's never read a book that wasn't about some popular cheerleader fighting back from a terrible disease, Brittany is the worst person to have as a study partner or member of your group project because she is totally not school smart and can't pay attention longer than it takes to brush her hair until it shimmers. What Brittany had going for her in the election was one very important factoid: Brittany was going steady with the most popular boy in the eighth grade, Bradley Duff—or Brad Dufus the Third, as Justine and I and our other best friends, Keisha and Gloria, call him. Brad Dufus the Third, who could intimidate the thirteen boys in our seventh-grade class with one strong-armed throw of a football, and who made the remaining girls in our class (besides me, Justine, Gloria, and Keisha, who know better) just swoon with "OhMyGod's." And the very fact that Brittany was the only person in our class to have an acknowledged boyfriend—who sat with her at lunch and played with her hair (when she wasn't brushing it), who walked her home from school—well, that was a very big obstacle of awe for me to overcome among the voting public, despite my admirable wardrobe and excellent report card.

So then Justine figured out a gimmick. I should become a vegetarian. Justine's mother is a political-science professor, and they decided I needed to run on an "issue" to combat the Brittany factor. Justine and her mom were right. Standing on a chair in the cafeteria, I proclaimed my new meat-free existence with a ceremonial dumping of spaghetti and meatballs into the garbage can. (It hurt, too. I really love meatballs.) The class liked that I respected their food choices and wanted to work to improve their lunch options in the cafeteria. Brad Dufus the Third was forgotten as ballots were cast in favor of a meat- and lactose-free cafeteria. So what that the cafeteria cooks told me to "fuggedaboutit" when I strutted into their kitchen as the newly elected seventh-grade president and demanded that our dietary needs be respected? What counted was that I made the effort, that I stayed a vegetarian on principle, and that my efforts at least resulted in lactose-free chocolate milk arriving in our cafeteria as a concession to my new political power.

Maybe it was a little radical to change my whole way of eating, but there is a price to be paid for popularity and being class president, and if that price is being a vegetarian, then I am willing to pay it.

So imagine my surprise and horror when I arrived at the Steps' house and they had cooked my supposed favorite chicken dinner.

I was so shocked I didn't know what to say. So I sat at the table and sulked.

Lucy said, "Annabel, do you like pizza? Dad says everyone in America loves pizza, and I want us to go together one night and eat pizza."

"I like pizza so long as it doesn't have sausage or anchovies on it," I said, thinking maybe they would get the message. And thinking, *STOP CALLING HIM DAD!*

"Me, too!" Lucy squealed. This girl was really getting on my last nerve.

"Annabel isn't eating her chicken, and Lucy is playing with her food," Angus whined. I had noticed very quickly that he was very competitive with Lucy. If Lucy had a game, he wanted to play it. If Lucy had a drink, he wanted a drink. If Lucy made a face at him, he couldn't wait to tell on her.

Jack was too distracted spoon-feeding Beatrice to notice.

Penny said, "Annabel, Jack cooks chicken cacciatore all the time and tells us how it's your favorite food. Lucy says it's her favorite food now too."

Lucy nodded and grinned at me. I could see that with a good makeover—replacing her corduroys with a funky plaid miniskirt, and taking away her sport top and replacing it with a soft cashmere short-cropped sweater—she could be quite the Miss Thang. With her rosy cheeks and big smile and athletic form, she would look great in my designs. Not like I'd ever let her know that.

My stomach growled. The chicken smelled sooo good, oozing with tomatoes and drowning in pasta. The food seemed to be calling to me, "Eat me, Annabel, sweet girl Annabel. You knooowwww how hungry you are. You remember how much you luuuuv chicken cacciatore." I nibbled at the potatoes on my plate, wanting to cry from how good the chicken smelled. *No one at the Progress School will know,* I thought. But I knew better. A guilty conscience would be harder to live with than Brittany Carlson herself taking my picture as I ate chicken cacciatore and then parading the photo all over school and saying, "See? I told you all you should have elected me class president, not Annabel. I wouldn't have said I was a vegetarian and then flown off to Australia and eaten chicken!" Horror!

"More mash, Annabel?" Penny asked.

"Mash?" I said.

"Mashed potatoes," Jack said, still not looking up from Beatrice's gooey vegetables dribbling down her sweet little face. *Angelina says you should never put pasta and mashed potatoes in the same meal. Too much starch.*

"No more," I said, "too much starch." I saw Jack's shoulders slump when I repeated that Angelina rule.

Penny said, "Is there anything special you want to do during your vacation with us?"

I ignored her and said, "Hey, Jack, do you remember how I sent you those E-mails about the class elections at my school?"

Jack finally looked away from Beatrice. "I think Penny asked you a question, young lady." *Young lady? What had they done to Jack?*

I couldn't take it anymore. I stood up and not-quite-yelled, "I'M A VEGETARIAN!"

Then I stormed away from the table and ran to Lucy's room, where they had put in a cot for me. I didn't care that it was her room. I slammed the door and lay down on the bed and cried. I looked up from my pillow once, and what I saw almost killed me. On Lucy's nightstand was a framed picture of Jack giving

Lucy a piggyback ride in some park. In the picture the sun reflected off her multicolored braces, her grin was that wide and happy. "He's *my* dad," I whispered.

I buried my head back into the pillow. I hated Australia, I hated the Steps, and I wanted to go home.

That was the first day.

Chapter 6

I woke up at about three in the morning, totally confused. I couldn't figure out where I was. The air from the open window was warm and balmy, and there was no street noise from taxicabs and buses. Moonlight was streaming in through the curtains, which freaked me out because I certainly didn't have smiley-face curtains hanging in my room in Manhattan! I could also see another bed next to mine. An empty bed, with . . . more smiley-face linens. *Blech*, I thought. At the Progress School we are so beyond smiley-face thingies everywhere. I realized I was still stranded in Sydney, Australia, and I was still mad about dinner. But where was Lucy?

I got out of bed and stumbled into the living room, where Jack was sitting in a big love-seat chair with a sheet draped over it for upholstery, which was the kind of house decorating Angelina always used to complain about when we lived with Jack. But all the furniture in his new house was homey and kind of tattered and worn in. Obviously, Penny didn't mind.

Jack was holding Beatrice and feeding her a bottle. "Anna-the-Belle," he whispered.

"Jack," I said. I crossed my arms over my chest.

"You fell asleep before I could come talk to you," he said.

I dropped my arms from my chest and sat down on the old sofa next to his chair. I could feel tears streaming down my face.

"I'm sorry, Annabel," Jack said. "You were right to be angry. I should have remembered you were a vegetarian. There are so many things going on here, sometimes I forget important details like that. I wanted everything to be perfect for you, and I blew it." He put down Beatrice's bottle and leaned in with his free hand to wipe away my tears.

"I guess I'm sorta sorry about yelling and running away," I whispered.

"Sorta?" He laughed softly.

"Sorta," I said, and laughed a little too. "Not totally." I caught my breath and added, "When you lived in New York, you never forgot about things like that. You were never that busy."

Jack said, "When I was in New York, I had a very unsuccessful career as a comedian, which left me with loads of time, and I was blessed with a daughter who remembered everything for me."

I liked that Jack was talking to me like he knew I wasn't a little girl anymore and I would understand what he was saying.

"And now?" I asked.

"And now," he said. He gestured toward the computer table, which was stacked with papers and glossy photos and baby toys and children's books. "And now I've got this moderately successful career as a booking agent, bringing comedians who are much funnier than I ever was over to Australia, and sending some Australian ones over to the States, and there's Lucy, Angus, and Beatrice . . ."

"Oh yeah—them . . ."

"Annabel, I know it's hard, but promise me you'll try. Lucy and Angus want so much for you to like them, they've been so excited about your coming here." He paused and looked into my face, like only he can do. Then he understood. "And you know you'll always be my best girl, and I'll always love you—"

"Love me best?" I interrupted.

Jack smiled. "Love you totally as my most wonderful, special, irreplaceable first daughter."

That was a start.

"So why don't you put down that baby already and make some room for me?"

Jack chuckled again and put sleeping Beatrice into the bassinet next to his chair. He held his arms out to me and I snuggled right in, resting on his lap and burrowing my head in his neck. It had been so long since

Jack had held me in his arms. He still smelled like aftershave and fresh garlic and tomatoes. He patted my head and twirled my hair as I sat in his lap.

"You're getting so tall!" he said.

"No I'm not, you're getting shorter!" I said. Our favorite old joke. After a few minutes of snuggling I asked, "Where's Lucy?"

"She went to sleep in Angus's room. But not before yelling at me for forgetting you were a vegetarian. She and Angus stayed up to make you something special."

"What?" I said it low and quiet so he would think I wasn't interested.

"Macaroni and cheese to eat tomorrow night. Your second-favorite meal, if memory serves. That was pretty cool of them, no?" I could smell the cheese sauce on Jack's shirt. I knew it was pretty cool of Jack, not of the Steps.

"I guess," I allowed. I didn't want to be mean about it, considering I had Jack all to myself.

Beatrice gurgled in her sleep. "Do you want to hold her?" Jack asked.

She was my half sister, not a step, so I figured why not. I lifted her out of the bassinet, careful to hold the back of her head, and the two of us sat with Jack in the big chair. She was so pretty, with eyes and lips shaped just like Jack's, and soft black hair just like Penny's. I could feel the rhythm of her breathing on my arm, which was cradling her back.

"Awesome," I whispered. I wondered if I could design baby clothes.

Feeling Beatrice's back rise and fall in my arms, cuddled in Jack's arms, I decided I felt okay about Beatrice and Jack. About Penny and the Steps, still not cool.

Chapter 7

When I woke up the second time, it was already noon! I have never slept so late in my life. Maybe I slept so late because I dreaded spending time with the Steps.

I was right to dread. The Steps, Jack, Penny, and Beatrice were all sitting around the kitchen table working on a giant puzzle of a panda, and obviously waiting for me to haul my butt out of bed. The first thing Angus said to me when I went into the kitchen was, "Annabel, the Frosties don't have any meat in them!"

"Frosties?" I mumbled, still dazed.

"Frosted Flakes, sleepyhead," Jack said. I have always been a Cocoa Puffs girl myself, so I didn't care about the Frosted Flakes.

"Bagel?" I asked.

"Penny went out and got you bagels this morning," Jack said. He said it like this was a special favor she had done for me, which I didn't like. They looked like such a family, and I felt uncomfortable that everyone was doing special things for me. I knew they were trying to be nice, and even though I didn't want to be part of their family, since I fully expected that Jack would come to his senses and come home to America, I still didn't appreciate being singled out with special treats, like I was a guest instead of a member of the family.

I made a face when I saw the bagel. It was pasty looking and small. I broke off a piece to sample. Dry, tasteless. Conclusion: Awful! If it's one thing I know besides clothes, it's bagels, and this was no New York bagel.

"How 'bout some of those Frosties?" I asked.

"You're a very picky eater," Lucy said.

"I have high standards," I answered back.

Frosties. Conclusion: Yuck! No wonder they didn't call the cereal by its proper name, Frosted Flakes. This cereal tasted nothing like what I expected from Tony the Tiger. The cereal tasted like sawdust sprinkled with sugar. I didn't know what scam these people in Australia were trying to pull, but their attempts at American breakfast foods were terrible, insulting even.

Jack said, "Nothing here seems to please you, Annabel. What would you like to have for breakfast?"

"How 'bout lunch?" I said. Because breakfast in Australia was a joke.

Angus said, "We could get Kinder Surprises from the milk bar! Annabel, Dad told me you don't have Kinder Surprises in America. It's this chocolate candy with a toy inside!"

I shrugged like that was no big deal. "Milk bar?" I said. "What's that?" *Milk bar?* What tilted kinda thing could that be?

"The store, silly!" Angus said. He shook his head and looked toward Jack like, *She doesn't know what a milk bar is?*

"It's a convenience store," Jack said. "Like the corner store or the neighborhood bodega."

"Oh," I said. "Milk bar" sounded to me like some cocktail lounge where cows sat on barstools and ordered some fancy drink on the rocks.

Penny butted in. "Lucy, how would you like to take Annabel into town for lunch? Just the two of you."

I figured Lucy would squeal with excitement, but now she shrugged her shoulders. She said, "Okay, I guess, if Annabel wants to go."

I totally did *not* want to go, but I looked at Jack's face, and he was staring at me with such hope, and I remembered I had promised him I would at least try.

"Well, okay, but only if you want to go," I said. I said the words in Lucy's direction, but I didn't actually look at her.

"Only if you want to go," Lucy said, this time in my direction but not to me.

"GO!" Jack and Penny said at the same time.

Chapter 8

This I will admit: Even though I was used to Manhattan skyscrapers and massive apartment buildings, I thought it was kind of cool that the Steps could live in a major city like Sydney, and yet their neighborhood, which was called Balmain, was really cozy and quiet, lined with pretty little Victorian cottages. As Lucy and I reached the top of the hills near the center of Balmain we could see the skyscrapers of the Sydney skyline and harbor. It was like being in Brooklyn, except the neighborhood felt very peaceful and, with its quaint cottages and willowy trees, somewhat enchanted.

At first Lucy and I didn't talk much. I don't know why she was so quiet. I knew I wasn't saying anything because I was mad about her stealing my dad, and because I had promised Justine that Lucy and I would never, ever become BFs. Justine was not happy about

Lucy or about my going to Sydney. (Justine conveniently forgot she was the one who had bailed on our Christmas vacation plans in the city because skiing was so much more fundamentally important than hanging out with her very best friend.)

Lucy was wearing navy Adidas running pants with the buttons on the side. She would have looked totally cute, except she was wearing a brown-and-orange-striped T-shirt with the name of some Australian football team on it. I was wearing a short white denim skirt with a scoop-necked navy tee that said NYC on it in big white letters. My tee would have looked perfect with her running pants.

As we strolled down the main street through Balmain we passed by several cool clothes shops that were selling leather skirts and feather boas and snakeskin-print blouses. I figured I'd better tell Jack to take Lucy shopping in these cool stores for her next birthday. These stores were ready for her fashion emergency.

Lucy led me into a small restaurant where you order at the counter. She stopped before we were all the way through the door and said, "They serve Mediterranean food here, like hummus and falafel and shish kebabs." She pronounced the word "ke-BAB" instead of "ke-BOB." "Is that okay with you, Miss Picky?" I could tell by her tone that she had figured out that I was not interested in being buds with her.

I stared into her baby blue eyes, the eyes I had been

35

studying so intently in pictures for months before coming to Australia. "I luuuv that kind of food," I said, so sugary sweet even I couldn't believe my ears.

Maybe she was relieved I wasn't being mean—or "ornery," as Bubbe says I can be sometimes—because Lucy seemed to sigh with relief. She obviously didn't understand sarcasm. She said, all excited, "There's loads of meatless foods here. I love this place. I can't believe Mum let us come all by ourselves!"

Just then, two girls just about our age walked into the restaurant and purposefully bumped into Lucy, spilling their Cokes on her T-shirt.

"Ooh, sorry!" one of the girls said. The girl totally did not mean it. Both of the girls were taller than Lucy and me, and while their outfits were much more put together than Lucy's, those girls were not nearly as pretty as she was. Maybe because they had the mean faces of bullies with nothing better to do than pick on people.

"Loser," the other girl muttered at Lucy, then she shoved Lucy and walked over to sit in a booth.

Lucy sprinted into the bathroom. I ran after her and found her crying over the sink.

Now was not the time for my attitude problem. "What was that all about?" I asked.

Lucy was crying really hard and wouldn't say anything. She just kept shaking her head and trying to bite back her tears, so her eyes and lips were getting really swollen.

I waited for her to answer, and when she didn't, I

wet down a paper towel and began wiping off her face. "You'd better tell me, or I'm going to tell your mom what just happened."

"Don't do that!" Lucy cried out.

"Then talk," I said. I patted her shoulder and promised myself I could do something "ornery" later to make up for this temporary truce.

"I don't know why they do that," Lucy said. "Ever since I came to school here, it has been horrible. The kids tease me about being from Melbourne and because I like Melbourne footy teams and they've all known one another since kindie and no matter what I do, it's wrong! I hate my new school! I hate Sydney!" She started crying all over again.

"Okay," I said, "first, you have to stop crying. I'm from New York, and I'm going to take care of this. But I need to know a few things first. How long have you been in this school?"

"For a year. Angus and I just finished our first year at our new school in Sydney. We moved up here this time last year."

She huffed a little but seemed to be calming down.

"Who's your best friend?" I needed to know, in case reinforcements were necessary.

"Her name's Jenny," Lucy sobbed all over again. "She lives in Melbourne. I don't have any friends here."

Her BF was in Melbourne. I knew that was way far away, at least a day's drive, because last year when Jack visited me in New York, he and Penny and the Steps were living in Melbourne, and he pointed it out to me on a map. Jenny in Melbourne would be no help to Lucy in Sydney.

"What are those girls' names outside?"

"Their names are Devon and Yasmin." *Beastly names for beastly girls*, I thought.

"Lucy," I said, "listen carefully. You just come back outside and follow my lead."

"I can't!" she wailed. "I can't go out there, so long as they're still there!"

"You can, Lucy, and you will. If you don't go back right now and show your face, they will only treat you worse. You can't let those dumb girls get the better of you."

I dug into my backpack and pulled out an extra T-shirt. Bubbe says always to carry a spare shirt and plenty of moist towelettes in case of emergencies.

"Put this on," I told Lucy.

"Really?" she said. She was finally interested in something other than those girls outside the bathroom. The spare tee was identical to the one I was wearing.

"Yes," I said. "You can't mess with fools like those girls if your outfit isn't properly coordinated."

"Oh," Lucy said. When she came out of the bathroom stall wearing the matching NYC tee, I saw, as I had suspected, that the shirt looked perf with her navy Adidas running pants. I pulled out a compact powder case Bubbe had given to me, and I tidied up Lucy's tearstained face.

When I was in fifth grade, when Jack first moved to Australia and Angelina and I moved in with Bubbe, I had to transfer from a school in Greenwich Village to the Progress School on the Upper West Side. The boys tried to trip me, and the girls never talked to me at lunch. It was terrible. I didn't know anybody except Wheaties, who had gone to the same nursery school as me, and let's just say having Wheaties as the only kid who knew me did not qualify me for popularity. Wheaties wasn't all bad, though. When no one wanted to eat lunch with me or pick me for kickball or dodgeball teams, Wheaties always tried to keep me company. He would sit with me at lunch and ask if I wanted a bite of his wheatgrass sandwich (as if!), or he would show me the liner notes of his favorite CDs when both of us were sitting on the bleachers during PE games. "You are so bizarre," I would say. "So?" he would say back.

At that time Justine was best friends with—get this!—Brittany Carlson, and Gloria and Keisha were inseparable, as they have been since first grade and probably will be until they're like thirty years old or something. Anyway, no one really talked to me, and I missed Jack so much, and I remember I was so miserable. Then one day the funniest thing happened. Brittany and Justine had a fight. What do you expect, though, when two such bossy people are best friends? Then Brittany asked a girl called Rebecca, who was meek and quiet and followed Brittany around like a puppy, to be her best friend. Soon after, Justine plopped herself down at the lunch table between me and Wheaties. She offered me half her PB&J sandwich and said, "So, you dress really cool and you seem pretty smart, do you want to be my best friend?" I nodded yes and after that my days trapped in the social dungeon were over. From that day forward I was accepted into the class at the Progress School. But I promised myself I would never forget those early months of fifth grade when I ran home from school every day and cried and was sure I'd never belong or have a best friend.

"C'mon, Lucy," I said. I grabbed her hand for a split second to make her feel strong.

I strutted right over to Devon and Yasmin's booth. They were guzzling Cokes and giggling.

"Scooch over, Devon, 'kay?" I said. I sat my bum inside the booth and nudged the bum of the girl with the gold necklace proclaiming DEVON in swirly rhinestone letters. That look is so '80s.

I could tell Devon was totally shocked, because her mouth kind of dropped and she moved over right away to make room for me.

"You too, Yasmin." I gestured my hand to Yasmin. "Make some room for my girl Lucy on your side."

"But . . . ," Yasmin started to sputter, completely confused.

"MOVE!" I said. I was firm but sweet. Yasmin jumped in her seat, then moved.

Lucy's face was horrified, like she wanted to yell *Stop, Annabel!* I shot her a look back: *Sit!* Lucy reluctantly sat down next to Yasmin, but at the farthest end of the seat, so her leg was practically dangling in the aisle.

"Ladies," I said. "How you doin'?" I talked in an exaggerated New York accent so I would sound like I was in a gangster movie. I pointed at Devon and then at Yasmin. "Lemme make somethin' clear here. You toucha my sister, I breaka you face." I was borrowing from a sign I'd seen in Little Italy in Manhattan: YOU PARKA IN MY SPOT, I BREAKA U FACE.

"You're not her sister," Devon accused. "She's from Melbourne, and you have an American accent!"

Lucy's courage found her. "Annabel is too my sister, she's my stepsister, but she is my sister and she's from America. See, she brought me this shirt from New York. She's from New York!"

"Wow," Devon and Yasmin said.

"And I'm here to tell you, lay off my sister." I laid on the New Yawk accent really thick.

Devon turned to me and asked, "Do you, like, know famous movie stars?"

"No," I said, forgetting all about my gangster voice. "But my best friend Justine knows Leonardo."

"OhmyGod!" Devon screamed, grabbing her hair. Well, okay, Justine was rollerblading once in Central Park and breezed right past some scruffy-wonderful guy who looked just like Leonardo. She wasn't positive that the beauty guy was Leonardo, but in her heart it was.

"Justine goes rollerblading with him in Central Park sometimes," I continued. "When he's in town."

Devon and Yasmin sat in stunned silence, practically drooling onto the table. They looked at Lucy with new appreciation. Yasmin asked Lucy, "How many times have you seen *Titanic*?"

Lucy didn't even know how horrible her answer was. I think she was so happy they were talking to her and not making fun of her. "Never, actually. It came out so long ago and our vid machine is always breaking, and we've been so busy, with moving from Melbourne and Beatrice being born, I just . . . I just . . . haven't seen it yet."

I was on Lucy's side, and even I was looking at her like her head had just sprouted tree branches. She couldn't be that hopeless—but she was! No wonder she was having a hard time at school. At the Progress School on the Upper West Side, boy bands and clothes styles come and go, but we will never, ever be over Jack Dawson, a.k.a. Leonardo, even if it came out like a million years ago.

Then I had a brilliant idea. I said, "Devon and Yasmin, why don't you guys come over so we can watch *Titanic* and you can explain all about Leonardo to my sister?"

They both looked kind of embarrassed, like, *What if someone sees us going into that weird girl from Melbourne's house?* I didn't exactly want to encourage Lucy's becoming friends with such jerky girls, even if they did love Leonardo the Most Beautiful, but I knew that if Lucy could become friendly with Devon and Yasmin, then other kids, better kids, would have the courage to talk to Lucy and be her friend. I fixed Devon and Yasmin with my coldest, most meanest New York squint-stare.

"Well, all right," Devon said quietly.

"When?" I demanded.

"Soon, I guess," Yasmin said, but you could tell she wasn't serious.

"Tell you what," I said. I scribbled the Steps' address on a napkin. "Here's our address. Come by tomorrow at noon, and we'll make popcorn and watch the movie."

"Your American accent is so cool," Yasmin said.

"You sound just like those people on the telly," Devon said.

They got up to leave. "We'll see you tomorrow?" I said.

"Yeah," they answered back. They both looked at Lucy. "Well, bye, Lucy," Yasmin said.

Lucy's face was flush with pleasure and relief.

"Bye!" she called out.

I might not have been pleased about the Steps, but so long as they were my family, no one was going to mess with them on my watch.

Chapter 9

Go figure. Lucy was titanically unimpressed with Leo. I almost—almost—admired her total freeze on Leo. "I don't see what the big deal is," she said after the movie. She said he totally was not cuter than Chandler on *Friends*, Lucy's favorite megastar guy. "Anyway," Lucy said, "Rose was the real hero of the movie, not Jack. She was the person I most admired in the movie."

Devon, Yasmin, and I sat on the pillows on the floor, drowning in popcorn and chocolate, with our tongues hanging out of our mouths. Did we hear Lucy correctly?

I thought, *Oh no, Lucy, don't say that in front of Devon and Yasmin when you finally have two almost-supporters in Sydney.* But I think that Devon and Yasmin, like me, were impressed that Lucy could be so strong and indifferent to Leonardo's charms.

"Wow," Devon said, "I never met any girl who wasn't absolutely crazed over Leo."

"You're like this anti-Leo girl," Yasmin said. She handed Lucy an invitation to a birthday party. I had seen the invitation in Yasmin's pocket all afternoon, and I knew she had been deciding all day whether or not to give it to Lucy. Maybe being anti-Leo made Lucy more interesting and mysterious to Devon and Yasmin. "So come by this party or something."

Yasmin's voice wasn't exactly enthusiastic about inviting Lucy, but she had invited Lucy nonetheless. Lucy's rosy face was pleased . . . and relieved. Like maybe she could see the light at the end of the social dungeon tunnel.

I wondered if it was Angus's fault that Lucy hadn't fallen under the Leo spell. That boy was one big pain. All through the first half of the movie he kept trying to distract us. He kept standing in front of the TV, smooching his lips together and making fish gurgle sounds, then he would wave and sway his arms like he was an octopus. Angus must be some kind of fishetarian. He just loves fish. It's the one food he won't eat, and all he ever wants to do is look at books about fish. Whatever! But his fishy behavior was a bit much. Finally, after Lucy shouted at him to bugger off, Penny made him go upstairs with her, Jack, and Beatrice. I think Penny was just happy that Lucy was having friends over.

"Is your brother always like that?" I asked Lucy

later, after Devon and Yasmin had left.

"Yeah, he's a huge, massive pain," Lucy said. Then she added, "And he's your brother too, you know."

That sounded too weird.

"He's my step," I said. "You're my step. That's all we'll ever be. Steps."

I remembered I had promised myself I could be mean to Lucy again once Devon and Yasmin were gone. Maybe she thought because I took up for her with Devon and Yasmin that we would be tight, but she was wrong. I was only temporarily helping out. And seeing Jack come downstairs after the girls were gone, carrying Beatrice, with Angus hanging on to his leg and Penny and Lucy gazing at him adoringly, I reminded myself that the Steps were not my friends.

Lucy looked like she was going to cry from what I had said. Instead she leaned over to whisper in my ear, so Jack and Penny would not hear her. "Sometimes I wish you weren't even my step. I wouldn't want you as my sister anymore. Your dad never warned us you'd be so stuck up."

Good, I thought. Now Lucy understood that I had no intention of being all cozy-cozy with her.

"Takes one to know one," I whispered back.

Jack and Penny looked at us, and Lucy and I both flashed brilliant smiles back at them, like we were going to be the bestest friends in the world. Not.

Chapter 10

Australia was the weirdest place. Rice Krispies were called Rice Bubbles, Popsicles were "icy pops," people said "ta" instead of "thank you," and everybody ended their sentences with "hey?" Like Angus would say, "I want an icy pop, hey? Ta." That was their "English." Another thing: Every time I went to the "milk bar" or the "veggie bar" (the vegetarian restaurant down the street), people imitated the way I talked. Like if I said, "I'll have an order of nachos," the waitress would repeat after me, in this exaggerated American voice, "Nah-chos." The first time I asked for guacamole, the waitress said, "What?" about five times and Lucy sat giggling at the table going "Guacamole, guacamole," in this ridiculous American accent. Apparently in Australia there is no word *guacamole*. They call it avocado sauce, and of course everybody laughed when I pronounced that, too. Lucy imitated me again, murmuring, "Ah-vah-cah-do," after me.

One time we were at McDonald's, when I asked for ketchup with my fries. Lucy said, "It's tomato sauce, not ketchup," but in her Australian pronunciation "ta-may-do" turned into "toe-mah-toe." When I gave her a look back like, *Well, excuse me!* she told me all about her letter-writing campaign to the ketchup-making companies asking that they start labeling the bottles with the "proper" name: tomato sauce. I was about to tell her she could take her girl power letter-writing campaign and shove it up her—but then Jack congratulated Lucy for taking "initiative" to write to those companies, so I shut up before I *really* said something mean. Instead I told Lucy, "In America, which probably invented ketchup in the first place, tomato sauce is a totally separate thing that you use to, like, make spaghetti sauce, so in America ketchup will always be the right word."

Angus was the worst. He kept laughing after I said I "brush" instead of "clean" my teeth, and he baited me all the time to recite the alphabet so he could laugh that I pronounced "zee" instead of "zed."

Penny told the Steps to stop imitating me because it was rude. They still did it when she wasn't around. They never teased Jack about his American accent. They were used to him, I guess. But something about hearing me made the Steps turn all giggly and rude.

Penny said I shouldn't be offended that people imitated the way I talked. She said it was because there was so much American television on in Australia that when people heard me speak, it was like I was a girl from *Friends* standing right in front of them. Sometimes Penny tried too hard to be cool—like I would want to be a girl from *Friends*, as if I were Brittany Carlson.

It was hard to like the Steps or Penny those first few days in Sydney. They were always hogging Jack and Beatrice. If I wanted to go swimming with Jack, Angus had to come too, because that boy loves water. If I wanted to go play catch with Jack, Lucy begged to come too, because she wanted to learn how to play American baseball. If I wanted to hold Beatrice, Angus and Lucy would crowd us and make faces at the baby and try to make her smile and laugh. If I wanted to hang out with just Jack, then Penny wanted him to help her change nappies or make dinner.

Besides, there was no time to have Jack to myself. Penny had our schedule for Christmas vacation planned out like she was a military general. She was so into *activities*. To me, activities were window-shopping on Madison Avenue, rollerblading in Central Park, or watching movies and eating popcorn with Justine, Gloria, and Keisha. Activities to me were not doing crosswords, making costumes, baking gingerbread-man cookies, and putting together endless puzzles.

On the third straight day of activities I asked Penny why we always had to be doing activities. I thought if I had to glue glitter onto one more greeting card, I was going to scream.

Penny looked so confused. "Well, with four children in the house, activities keep us on schedule and keep everybody settled."

Schedule? Settled? Lucy and I counted as *children*? Hello, we were practically *thirteen*!

Jack was in another room changing Beatrice's nappy, so I did not hesitate to answer back fresh to Penny. "I am not a child, Penny. And I do not like activities and I will not do them any longer. Back in New York, before you knew Jack, we used to go places. We did not always stay cooped up in the house doing activities. I want to go somewhere." Penny's face looked very hurt, so I did not add, *And I know we always have to do activities because you don't want me to have Jack all to myself and steal him back. You want to hold us all here as captives so no one will have the chance to see that this "family" totally does not work.*

I could see Lucy's lips curl into a smile under the mask she was making. She and her mom had been fighting at night before bed, when they thought I couldn't hear them yelling at each other upstairs in Jack and Penny's room. From what I had overheard, Lucy was mad because every year after Christmas, Lucy and Angus spent a week at their grandmother's house in Melbourne—their grandmother who was the mom of their real dad. And this year, because I was here, Penny said they couldn't go. But I knew that Penny was using me as an excuse. I had heard Penny talking on the phone to Lucy's grandma, and her tone was very annoyed and angry. Penny and Lucy's grandma didn't get along. This I understood. Bubbe and Jack have never gotten along. Bubbe thinks it's Jack's fault that he and Angelina never got married. But I was there when Jack and Angelina were living together, and I know it was Angelina who didn't want to get married, not Jack. Can't tell that to Bubbe, though. Bubbe hears only what she wants to hear, as Angelina reminds me all the time.

"What would you like to do, then, Annabel?" Penny asked. She did not snap at me the way Angelina might have for being fresh. Her tone was phony-nice, like she was trying to prove she knew I knew I would never think of her as my mom, and she was trying too hard to be my cool stepmom.

Before going to Australia, I had been pouring over *Vogue* magazines and reading up on Sydney on the Internet. I knew just what I wanted to do. "I want to go to the market at Paddington and to the clothes shops on Oxford Street and to the Strand shopping arcade."

Lucy's jaw dropped, I swear. This was probably, aside from the Devon-Yasmin incident, the most I had said around Penny and the Steps since I arrived.

I could tell Penny was trying really hard not to be mad at me. I figured this must have been hard for her, since she and Lucy had been fighting so much, so I appreciated her—a little—for trying. She said, extra patiently, "I was under the impression you weren't too impressed with Sydney and weren't too interested in going about much. I asked you when you first got here if there was anything special you wanted to do, and you didn't answer me. Why didn't you say something earlier?"

Lucy knew the answer. Lucy said, "Because you made meat for dinner!"

I took the high road. I didn't acknowledge that Lucy was right.

Chapter 11

The next day I learned right away why Penny liked to stick to activities at home. Dragging around Angus and Beatrice was a major pain.

When we finally got sprung from the Steps' cottage in Balmain, we rode a ferry to the other side of Sydney Harbour. From the boat I could see the Sydney Opera House, which looked like this gorgeous whitewashed fan streaking the blue sky. It was incredible looking. The subway in Sydney was pretty cool too, I have to confess. It wasn't ultranoisy like the subway in Manhattan, and the train cars had three different levels, like they were their own underground moving building!

I couldn't complain about walking around in December in shorts and sandals, either. That sun was bliss and provided great fashion opportunities for short skirts and platform sandals, glittery tank tees . . .

and hats! Everybody in Australia wears hats, Jack told me, because the hole in the ozone layer exposes people in Australia to skin cancer more than in any other place. Angus wore the cutest kind of hat that all the young schoolchildren wear in Australia, bright cotton with a brim in the front and flaps hanging over the ears. Penny and Lucy wore plain straw hats, but I didn't let on that I thought they looked nice, if boring. Jack wore his beloved New York Mets cap, which he also wears inside the house when he's not even trying to protect his face from skin cancer.

Seeing all those fabu hats made my first shopping mission clear. *Hats, here I come,* I thought as we wandered from the subway station to Paddington Market. If you think going hat shopping in an open-air market would be an easy task, think again. One word: Angus! He would not stop fidgeting around, and if he wasn't fidgeting, he was running through stalls and knocking things over. When Lucy scolded him, he told her he would behave only if she promised to give him some "chockie," which is Australian for chocolate. Lucy told Angus to kiss off. Then every time Angus "settled" (as Penny called it), Beatrice started crying, needing to be fed, or throwing up. *Oy vey!* Being freed from Penny's activities was proving not fun at all.

Finally I said to Jack, "Can we go off on our own?" He looked to Penny, who nodded reluctantly. Penny told him she would take Angus and Beatrice to Baskin-Robbins, and we could meet them there in an hour. Which of course meant Lucy was stuck with us. Double ugh!

Jack mouthed the words *thank you* to Penny, like Penny was doing him some favor by letting him spend actual time with his actual daughter. Jack smiled really wide and took my and Lucy's hands on either side of him. "An hour with my best girls," he said. Behind his back I stuck my tongue out at Lucy. She didn't see.

The clothes displayed in the stalls were supremely funky and outrageous: loads of narrow-cut sweaters, hip straight skirts with side slits, retro bell-bottoms, and wild-patterned leather boots. Jack explained that Paddington Market is where a lot of young and upcoming fashion designers get their start. *Sydney's not such a bad place at all,* I thought. In fact, I thought the city—if you took away Penny and the Steps—was pretty amazing. Especially when I saw the small designer shops on nearby Oxford Street, which sold the totally cutest, most unique dresses, sweaters, and skirts I ever saw (and that included Bloomingdale's, my most favorite store ever).

I thought it was too bad Jack was going to have to return to America with me, because I realized I could get used to this Sydney clothes scene, and I would not mind at all eventually making clothes that could be displayed in places like Paddington Market and Oxford Street.

I bought the most cool vintage brown cowboy hat,

with beads hanging down from the rim on each side and a bowling-shirt-type letter *A* stenciled on the front. "That hat's the most dreadful thing I ever saw," Lucy said. That comment, of course, sealed the sale.

Jack laughed when he saw me wearing the hat, which was a great match with my overall shorts and surf T-shirt. "That's my Annabel!" he said. "Oh, when your Bubbe sees you wearing that . . ." He laughed all the way to Baskin-Robbins as I piggybacked on his back and looked down at Lucy's boring ole straw hat and thought, *Hopeless.*

Chapter 12

I was falling in love with Sydney, Australia, so I almost thought it was a shame that I was going to have to inform Jack that he absolutely, positively needed to move back to America where he belonged, with me. I was loving Sydney so much, even the Steps didn't seem so bad. Over the next couple of days I actually started to like them okay. Not love-adore-let's-spend-every-minute-together them, but they got on my nerves less.

Like Angus. Who knew that he could be so fun at museums? At the modern-art museum he stood in front of the paintings and sculptures, rubbing his chin with his hand, like he was a professor stroking his beard and thinking up some totally smart thing to say. And when I laughed at him, he giggled too and impulsively hugged my leg. "I like you, Annabel," he said. I think he meant like-like, too! I never heard of anyone having their first crush on their step, but all righty then, Angusfreak. At the aquarium at Darling Harbour (his favorite place) he knew everything about every last moving creature in water. I never knew a five-year-old could know so many facts. He'd be great to have around in biology class. Most fun was watching Angus stare intently at the different fish species and then try to imitate the way they swam or the way their faces looked. Even Lucy was giggling, and Angus probably annoys her the most of anybody.

Lucy had her moments too. At the Strand Arcade—which is this gorgeous shopping mall, but not like a mall in America, because it is a building of two narrow stories with gilt trim and crystal lights everywhere and small boutiques selling the coolest clothes and jewelry—Lucy grabbed my hand and dragged me into a sewing shop. The tiny shop was covered wall-to-wall with beautiful fabrics and laces and braided trim. Lucy went right to the drawers of sewing patterns. "Let's choose one!" she said.

"But why?" I said.

"So we can make something together," she said, like of course I should have known that.

"But I don't know how to sew," I said.

Her baby blue eyes were wide with shock. "But I thought you said you wanted to be a fashion designer."

"I do."

"And you don't know how to sew?" Lucy said it like I was some kind of idiot.

"No." It had never occurred to me even to try. I just liked to draw designs; shop, shop, shop; pick outfits for Angelina, Justine, Gloria, and Keisha; and look at the pictures in *Vogue* and *W* magazines like those magazines were the Bible. "You know how to sew?" I asked her. I said it like it was no big deal.

"Of course," she said. *Of course.* That was such a stuck-up answer, I thought. "My Granny Nell taught me. We were going to work on a special party dress for me this holiday. Until you had to come."

Her eyes stared right into mine, accusing. I guess I felt a little bad that she thought that, even though I knew it wasn't my fault she wasn't visiting her grandmother, so I said, "Maybe you could teach me how to sew?"

Her face turned bright pink happy. "That would be so fun!" she said. The thing about Lucy was, all I had to do was be a little nice to her to make her so happy. And considering that she had had a miserable first year in Sydney, that she couldn't see her Granny Nell, and that she was pretty funny every night when she brushed her teeth and sang "Spice Up Your Life," her mouth filled with toothpaste and her eyes laughing, shaking her hips and gurgling, "Shake it to the left! Spice up your life!" so that she almost made me like the Spice Girls again, I figured I could do this favor for her and let her teach me to sew.

One day we drove over to Bondi Beach (pronounced "Bond-eye"). I couldn't believe it, but Lucy knew how to surf, too. Even Justine, who can rollerblade across Central Park faster than anyone you ever saw and who can do cartwheels all up and down Fifth Avenue, cannot surf.

The beach was beautiful, with tons of kids hanging around, wearing the most excellent surf clothes and bathing suits I've ever seen. The only beach I'd ever been to before was in Miami with Bubbe, but that was pretty boring. Mostly Bubbe sunned herself on a beach chair, drinking cocktails and smoking and talking to other old people, and I would end up floating in the water on a raft and counting the minutes until we went back to New York. But Bondi Beach! It was swarming with kids and music and fun. And I couldn't believe I could be enjoying such incredible weather at the end of December.

"Who taught you how to surf?" I asked Lucy as we sunbathed on the beach by ourselves. Jack, Penny, Angus, and Beatrice had gone for a walk to get ice creams.

"My dad. My real dad," Lucy said. She was wearing sunglasses, so I couldn't tell whether talking about her real dad was going to make her cry. There was a girl in my third-grade class whose mother had died of cancer. The girl used to cry a lot, and she hardly talked to anyone ever, until finally her dad took her out of school and home-schooled her until she could get better. I knew that even though I was mad about Jack's moving to Australia, I was still lucky to have a dad.

"Do you remember your real dad?" I asked Lucy. I guess we must have been getting comfortable with each other, because I didn't feel weird about asking, and she didn't seem to feel too weird about answering.

"Totally," she said. "He wasn't funny like your dad, or tall, and he was older. He was very kind and sweet. We read fairy books together every night. He taught me how to surf. He loved the ocean. I think Angus gets that from him. Except Angus never knew our dad. But he looks just like him."

"Do you miss him?"

She took her sunglasses off and locked her eyes with mine. "Of course," she said. That *of course* again, except this *of course* wasn't stuck up. It was sad and painful. I understood that, like me, the day didn't go by that she didn't think about and miss her dad. I guess I minded a little less that she had borrowed Jack for a while. Lucy and Angus needed some Jack too.

Chapter 13

We were almost cozy, me and the Steps. For like a day.

It was New Year's Eve day, and we were all going to stay at home. Penny and Jack needed a quiet day after all the running around of the past few days.

Jack had dug into the garage (or car port, as they call it in Australia) and found Lucy's grandmother's sewing machine in a box that hadn't been unpacked yet. It didn't even take him too long to find the box. He had everything in the garage categorized, labeled, and organized by size and weight. This was not the Jack I remembered when he lived with Angelina and me. That Jack was confused a lot of the time, disorganized, and miserable from fighting with Angelina. The Australia Jack was not incompetent, as Angelina and Bubbe said. This Jack could cook using metric measurements, he could drive on the left side of the road, he could soothe a screaming baby. And when

Lucy saw that sewing machine sitting on her desk in her room, Jack was her hero.

"I'm so glad you're becoming friends with Lucy," Jack said to me privately. "She's had a tough time since we moved from Melbourne." I raised my eyebrows at him. Who said we were becoming friends? Lucy and I were more like schoolmates from different cliques who had no choice about working on a history project together. I had only gotten to the point where I could barely tolerate her. That was all.

Lucy set up the sewing machine on the desk in her room. Yes, the desk was plastered with sappy smiley faces and flowers, but it was a nice desk otherwise, painted a really cool yellow color with white trim. "My real dad made this desk," Lucy told me. She opened a desk drawer and showed me some Barbie clothes her Granny Nell had helped her make years earlier on the same sewing machine, at the same desk.

I had been staying in her room for a week, but I never felt like it was a room we shared. It was so totally her space, her things. And I was very into brown and gray that season and would never decorate my room in colors like yellow and pink.

"Wouldn't it be neat if I could have bunk beds and we could share this room?" Lucy asked. We were both standing over Beatrice and cooing at her. The baby was asleep on Lucy's bed. Penny and Jack were taking a nap with Angus. They had let Lucy and me baby-sit Beatrice all by ourselves. "And then when Beatrice is older, we could add another bed for her. And we'd all be, like, sisters in the same room."

I may have steps and a half sister, but I will always consider myself an only child. And only children never share rooms.

"Do you have a boyfriend?" I asked Lucy.

She whispered in my ear, "I liked this boy when I first came to Sydney. He was in my class. He was from America. His name was Bo. He was from a place called Atlanta. Everybody made fun of him, too. But then his family moved back to the States last July. He sends me E-mail sometimes!"

"You don't have to whisper in my ear," I said. "No one's around."

Lucy giggled and blushed. She pulled a picture out of her desk drawer of a geeky-looking boy wearing an Atlanta Braves T-shirt and a goofy, sweet grin. "I know," she said shyly. "Is there any boy you like?"

"All the cute boys from my school graduated into ninth grade. I like high school boys." It was true. There were no boys in my class or the eighth-grade class even close to dreamy. They were all either scrawny and peculiar, like Wheaties, or lost to their PlayStations. It was so distressing. I couldn't wait for high school.

Lucy really knew what she was doing with that sewing machine. After measuring a sleeping Beatrice, she cut a piece of plain blue cotton fabric and sewed together the body of a simple dress for Beatrice.

"Next, we can sew on some buttons and stuff, and then we'll make the sleeves," she said.

She tried to show me how to thread the needle, but I kept pricking myself. I was no more successful when Lucy tried to show me how to work the pedal on the sewing machine. I also couldn't keep track of where to put the fabric under the needle.

"How 'bout if I am the designer, and you be the seamstress?" I asked. I didn't want her to see me struggling to do a craft she was obviously great at.

"That's a good idea," Lucy said. I got my white sketch pad and pencils from my suitcase. She put on the radio, and we sat together for almost an hour, her sewing, me drawing, Beatrice sleeping.

Penny came in, still a little groggy from her nap. "What a nice picture," she said. She went to the living room and came back with her camera and started snapping pics of us. Penny is a really good photographer. The neat thing about her photos is they're not simple portraits. People are always in action in her pictures: the Steps looking like they're floating through space in a shot of them riding swings, laughing and waving; Lucy coming out of the ocean in her wet suit, carrying her surfboard, a face of pure joy and concentration from having caught an excellent curl; Angus staring through the glass at an octopus at the aquarium, totally mesmerized; Jack sitting in the rocking chair, feeding Beatrice, with a lazy smile on his face, and both of them asleep. Penny's pictures are framed and plastered all over the house. She only photographs in black and white. She has a job as an aerobics instructor, but really she would like to one day make money from her photographs. I'll give her this: She's major talented. She could make money from her pictures.

Angus came in, totally energized from his nap. He heard the radio playing and asked, as he always does whenever pop music is playing, "Is this hit from the seventies, eighties, or nineties?" He then ripped through Lucy's room, knocking over a tin of buttons, dragging a spool of thread across the room, shouting, and laughing. "Take my picture, Mum! Take my picture!" Penny was so involved in her picture taking, she did not yell at Angus for being so wild. Somehow, though, for once Lucy and I did not care. He was so funny. We laughed and started decorating Lucy's room with beads and buttons everywhere, and we ran around the beds waving ribbons, and when Beatrice woke up, she didn't cry, she laughed, and you could tell she recognized us and was glad we were playing around her.

Then Jack joined the party. When he came inside Lucy's room, Angus pointed at me and said, "Annabel, now you take Mum's camera, you take some pictures so we can have pictures of just our family."

Just our family. That's when the fun ended. I got the message.

Chapter 14

I will not say that I had begun to like the Steps. No way, no day. Appreciate them, occasionally. But no matter what, I just never felt totally comfortable in their house. Their accent was weird. The food never tasted right. The television programs looked all wrong. I knew I didn't belong. Like when I was offering to help with the dishes, and Penny said, "Thank you, Annabel, but you're our guest. Lucy and I will do the dishes." See what I am saying? Angus's wanting me out of the family picture only confirmed that feeling.

So by the end of the first week, even though I had come to love Sydney, I was ready to go home. I missed talking to Justine every night on the phone. I missed sitting on the floor at Angelina's feet before bedtime, watching Nick at Nite as Angelina braided my hair for bed. I missed going clothes shopping with Bubbe and then sharing a gigantic chocolate sundae with her afterward, surrounded by shopping bags. I missed the energy of New York, the lights in all the buildings glowing in the crisp winter air, and the doormen at our building slapping me five as I came home from school every day. I missed home.

So finally, on the night of New Year's Eve, I laid it all out to Jack. I was supposed to be in Sydney for only four more days, so I figured I had better make my case so Jack would have time to prepare.

For once I had Jack to myself. Angus and Beatrice were in bed. Lucy and Penny were upstairs fighting again. I think working on her Granny Nell's sewing machine had made Lucy mad all over again about not getting to spend some of her holiday with her grandma. I would have been mad too.

So Jack and I were sitting on that big chair again, me in his lap, only this time we weren't making up from a fight.

"Jack," I said. I rested my head on his chest. "We need to talk. I think it's time you move back to New York."

I could hear his heartbeat quickening. "That's pretty funny, Annabel," he said.

I lifted my head and shook it so he would see I wasn't kidding. He put his hand under my chin and rubbed it.

"You know I can't do that, sweetheart," he said.

"Why?" I could feel tears coming.

"I have a family here," he said. "I like it here."

He couldn't come home because he liked it here? How insulting to me! That was it. "WELL, I DON'T LIKE YOU BEING HERE!" I yelled.

"Don't yell, young lady," he said, startled. It wasn't like my yelling would bother anyone. Lucy and Penny were yelling much louder upstairs.

"You like them better!" I said. I started to cry for real. I hadn't factored into my equation that Jack would have absolutely no interest in moving home where he belonged. "You forgot all about me."

He tried to grab me into a hug, but I jumped from his lap and shoved him away.

"That's not true, Annabel," he said. "How could you think that?"

"They call you Dad! They get to see you every day! The only way you remember me is by my school picture on the refrigerator."

He sat down next to where I had scrunched myself into a ball on the sofa and he rubbed my back. "Annabel, you're one of the most important people in the world to me. You don't know how hard it was leaving you and moving here."

"You seem to have done it pretty okay!" I said.

He stopped rubbing. I could tell I had hurt him. I was glad.

"Annabel, you were the only part of my life in New York that was good. I wasn't happy there. And there was another part of my heart, and that's Penny. You don't know how many times I have wished that you could be here too, so all the pieces could be in place. But that's not always possible."

I repeated my original point. "I think you should move back to New York."

He had let me get in one mean comment, but he wasn't going to let in another. "Enough," he said, and I knew he meant it. "Besides, what would you have me do about Penny, Lucy, Angus, and Beatrice?"

"They could come to New York too." I thought this was a pretty generous thing of me to say.

Jack said, "Would it surprise you to know that Penny and I considered that option?"

I nodded. I was surprised. Seemed to me like they had just decided to live their lives without consulting me, or Lucy, and asking what we thought the best options were.

Jack continued, "New York is a very expensive city. And Lucy and Angus have already gone through so much, Penny thought it would be too much of a move to take them so far from home. Besides, I love it here. I'm happy here. Can you understand that? Penny and I hoped that you would like it here and maybe you would consider spending part of the year, during your summer and Christmas holidays, with us in Sydney. Be a part of this family, as well as the family you have with Bubbe and Angelina."

"Then, why do you always treat me like a guest?" Jack looked totally shocked by my question.

I never got a chance to hear Jack's answer. The phone rang. Jack answered it. The voice on the other end pained him even more than what I had just been telling him. His face took on that confused, sad, irritated look I remembered from Manhattan.

He handed the phone to me. "It's your mother," he said. "We'll finish this conversation in the morning, young lady." What was up with the "young lady" business? Jack was only in his mid thirties. This new language was way too radical for someone so young. Australia and too many children had turned Jack into one big S-Q-U-A-R-E.

Jack went upstairs, his shoulders slumped. Angelina also walks away in misery after she talks to Jack on the phone. Whatever is between them, they hate having to talk to each other.

"Angelina!" I said into the phone. I was so excited to hear her voice, I didn't care about the tears that had just been pouring down my cheeks.

"Baby, baby, baby!" she screamed. The cutest thing about Angelina is that when she is excited, she talks a mile a minute. Also, you never met anyone who loves talking on the phone as much as Angelina. One time while she was waiting in a hallway for an audition, she was talking to me on her cell phone. The audition was for a telephone commercial, and she got the part because the producers heard her yammering on the phone outside their offices, and when they came outside to hear who was making all the noise, they were amazed that someone could be that pretty and also so excited about talking on the phone. Justine, Gloria, and Keisha still call Angelina "the fast-talking telephone lady" because for a while you could not turn on your TV and not see Angelina selling you a long-distance service.

"You're not going to believe what I have to tell you!" Angelina squealed.

"What time is it there?" I asked her. I was used to talking to Jack on the phone from another hemisphere, but not Angelina. It seemed hard to believe that she could be in Hawaii, thousands of miles away, across an ocean and above the equator, and I could hear her like she was standing next to me.

"It's late night here. But I couldn't wait to tell you what happened. Harvey proposed! We're getting married!"

I was so shocked I didn't know what to say. This was welcome news—*not!* It was one thing to date Wheaties' dad, but to marry him? And not ask me first? This felt worse than Jack moving to Australia.

"Annabel? Are you there?"

"I'm here," I said, very quiet.

"Are you happy for me, baby?" *Happy for you?* I thought. *What about happy for me?* I hadn't even gotten used to Penny, the Steps, and a new baby half sister. I wasn't ready to go through it all over again. I still hadn't recovered from the first round.

"I guess," I said. *NO!* I thought.

"It's a big change, I know, Annabel baby, but it's

going to be great. GREAT! We've set a date for the wedding for next month, and I want you to be my maid of honor. I thought you could design the dress yourself and we could take it down to the Lower East Side to be made and as soon as you get home we'll go shopping for my bridal dress and Bubbe is so excited you would not believe it she flew to Hawaii to look at bridal magazines with me and make wedding arrangements—you know how she's been dying for a wedding—and guess what else?"

Angelina must have known I wasn't going to be totally thrilled by her news because if Bubbe had already flown from Florida to Hawaii to be with her, then Angelina must have known she was getting married for several days before calling to tell me.

"What else?" I said, but I thought I already knew. Harvey had just proposed and they were having a wedding in a month? This whole deal was so *90210*.

"You're going to be a big sister! We're having a baby next summer! And Harvey wants to buy a new apartment big enough for all of us—"

This is how mad I was: I hung up the phone, then unplugged it so she could not call me back.

I went into Lucy's room and lay down on the cot. Lucy was sitting on her bed, sewing lace trim onto a sleeve for Beatrice's dress.

"Parents are so stupid," I said.

"I don't know what is wrong with those people," Lucy added.

"I've had it," I announced. Whatever happened to normal parents who first got married and then had children, who stayed together, had regular jobs, and didn't traipse around all over the world bringing new steps into their children's lives?

Lucy put down her sewing and jumped onto my cot. Beads from that afternoon's play sprayed onto the floor. She grabbed my hand and said, "Then, let's do something about it."

Chapter 15

I never thought Lucy would have the guts to pull off such a stunt.

I was wrong. Way wrong.

I woke up the next morning, seated upright, my body gently rocking. As I opened my eyes I saw a conductor walking through the . . . train aisle? "Last stop, Melbourne, ten minutes," the conductor said.

Melbourne? Huh? Where was I? And why was Lucy's sleeping head on my shoulder? I looked down at the light weight I felt on my chest as I breathed—and when did I get well-developed boobies?

Then I remembered. Lucy and I had run away. She had masterminded an incredible escape. We would be arriving in Melbourne to visit her Granny Nell any minute.

We had started the night before by walking in on Jack and Penny, who were making out on the sofa in the candlelit living room. They were listening to sexy soul music, and they obviously didn't remember that Lucy and I were both mad at them. "Good night," we called out over the mood music. "Happy New Year!" They were so into each other they didn't even look up. And can I tell you that it was just past eight o'clock in the evening, and they didn't even notice that we were saying good night so early? Disgusting.

We placed a sign on Lucy's bedroom door that said, PLEASE DO NOT DISTURB US UNTIL TOMORROW MORNING OR YOU WILL RUIN OUR SCIENCE PROJECT. THAT MEANS YOU, ANGUS! As an extra precaution we placed pillows under our blankets in the shape of sleeping bodies. Lucy figured it would be after breakfast before anyone even noticed we were gone.

Lucy pulled out two short dresses from her closet. She handed me Kleenex to fill our training bras. We also dug into a pile of Penny's discarded makeup, and we applied lipstick, eyeliner, and eye shadow.

"Just trust me," she said. "We're teenagers going to a New Year's party. Play the part."

We climbed out her bedroom window and walked toward the ferryboat station. "My feet hurt, I can't walk anymore," I said. Lucy had also made me wear a pair of play high heels. "Can't we take a cab to the train station instead of the ferryboat?"

"Genius, we're twelve years old. We don't have loads of money." Lucy's hair was moussed up into a blond skyscraper.

"I do," I said. Bubbe had given me a wad of emergency money at the airport in New York. She said it was for an "emergency," but we both knew it was for shopping. And in Australia, because of the currency exchange rate, I actually had almost a third more money than Bubbe had given me. I put my fingers in my mouth and whistled like I was in New York again. Ten minutes later a cab came by after dropping some passengers off up the street.

"Bubbe always says to put your money where your mouth is," I told Lucy.

She rolled her eyes and got in the cab.

Lucy directed the driver to the train station. He looked into the rearview mirror twice, trying to decide whether or not we were old enough to be in a cab going to the train station on New Year's Eve.

Lucy pushed out her new bosom and said to me, for the cab driver to hear, "Like, I am so totally excited about James's party! Like, I am going to get so totally wasted and totally make out with him all night when the clock strikes midnight. Like everyone is going to be at this party!" She pulled—get this!—a *cigarette* out of her purse and leaned toward the front seat. She asked the driver, "Mind if I smoke in here?"

My eyes almost burst out of their sockets. I remembered that Lucy had said she wanted to be an actress, but I had no idea she could be this good.

"Yeah, I do mind," the driver said. But he drove on.

I decided to play the game with Lucy. "Like, I am totally having the most major sweet sixteen party for my birthday this year!" I tried to talk in an Australian accent too. I wasn't half bad.

Lucy said, "I had one for mine. Sixteen was such a great birthday. Now that I'm almost seventeen, my mum goes, she goes, 'So, like, how do you want to celebrate?' and I go, 'Like, with my friends, okay?' because I am so tired of having birthday parties with my parents around."

The driver stopped looking at us in the rearview mirror.

We had to run from the cab to catch the overnight train to Melbourne. We might not have gotten past the train conductor at the platform, who was directing people to their seats, if it had not been for the middle-aged couple who were totally drunk, standing ahead of us in line to board the train. "Dad's totally trashed," Lucy whispered to the train conductor as she showed him our tickets, the tickets she and Angus were supposed to use before it was decided I was coming to visit Australia instead. "Please excuse him." She blushed as if on cue. Impressive!

"I'm your father now, eh?" the drunk man slobbered.

"Shut yer trap!" the woman yelled at him.

Lucy and I both put on our most embarrassed looks. "They do this every New Year's Eve," Lucy mumbled to the conductor.

The train conductor shook his head with contempt for our "parents" and concern for us. "I've got two seats open in first class if you two good girls want to get a good night's sleep and let those two sleep it off in economy."

"Oh, yes please!" Lucy said.

"Do you think they'll be okay if we leave them alone?" I asked her. I scrunched my face into a worried look.

"Mum and Pop can take care of themselves! I've had enough of this!" Lucy said. She stomped toward first class as the train conductor shook his head at our "parents."

First class was nice (it didn't actually look that different to me from economy, but I was impressed all the same), but it wasn't like the extra seat space meant we would get any extra sleep. The adults riding in the car were drinking champagne and chattering, waiting for that "10-9-8-7-6-5-4-3-2-1, Happy New Year" thing.

Once the conductor left us alone at our seats, we burst out laughing for about fifteen minutes straight. We almost fell out of our chairs from laughing. If I had been drinking a Coke, I would have been snarfing it all over our seats. I don't think I've ever laughed that hard with Justine, Gloria, or Keisha.

"We are toooooo smooooooth," I giggled.

"Oh, we were the bomb!" Lucy laughed. She got that expression from me. Nobody in Australia says that.

After we stopped laughing, we sat side by side, silent for a few minutes, as if we were both wondering, *Now what?* When we shared her room, we rarely said much to each other. Well, when I first arrived, Lucy had talked a lot, but she had figured out pretty quickly from my silence that I did not want to be chatterbox queen with her.

"When do you think they'll figure out we're gone?" I finally asked her, to break the silence.

Lucy shrugged. "I don't care." I knew she was lying.

I felt kind of freaky. As the train raced from the suburbs into the countryside, I pressed my nose against the window so I could see the landscape outside without the light reflected from the train car. Pitch-black darkness, with occasional bursts of street, house, or farm lights, whizzed by. Loud adults, drinking and smooching, partying, made the train ride seem especially weird and lonely. They did not notice us at all. Suddenly, I was scared. I had never been farther from Manhattan than Miami, and now I was a continent and a hemisphere away, a runaway, on a train bound for endless black sky.

Lucy seemed to sense my nervousness. She handed me a blanket and wrapped it over me. "We're okay," she said very softly. Then she asked if I wanted anything to eat. I shook my head. "Well, I'm starving!" she said.

She left for the food car and came back carrying Cokes and "pasties" (pronounced "PAH-stees" in

Australianese), which are these weird pastry rolls filled with meat or vegetables, and which I had detested when I first arrived but had come to like a lot.

"I'm surprised you didn't come back with beers, too, Miss Actress," I said. Lucy giggled.

"Need the pasties to grow up and out." She jutted out her chest, and we started laughing all over again.

"My Bubbe and I were in Bloomingdale's buying my first bra, and she told the saleslady that my chest was 'perky'! I almost died right there," I confessed to Lucy.

"If you think that's bad, I heard my mum talking on the phone to her best friend and she told her friend that I had started my period and then described my bozzies as 'gorgeous.' Can you believe that?" Lucy blushed at the memory.

"Your 'bozzies'?" I asked.

Lucy pointed at her bosom. That *ie* thing again.

"You started your period?" I whispered.

"Uh-huh, three months ago. I thought I would be happy about it, but really it's a drag. I feel all cramped up and hungry all the time." Lucy was not bragging about having started her period, the way Justine does. You would think that periods were invented just so Justine could tell you, "I've had mine, you know."

I'm still waiting for mine. At least I could console myself—my Kleenex bozzies were bigger than Lucy's.

Lucy shivered from the cold train air. I extended the blanket to her. We sat huddled under the blanket, maybe a little uncomfortable that we were telling each other private things.

"What's your mum like?" Lucy asked after another spell of silence.

That was hard to answer. Before that call from Hawaii, Angelina had been one of my favorite people in the whole world. Now I wanted to shut her out of my mind. I was running away so I wouldn't have to think about the wedding, about Harvey, Wheaties, or another half sibling. And I especially didn't want to think about moving in with those people. I liked living with Bubbe.

I pulled a picture of Angelina out of my backpack and handed it to Lucy. It was one of Angelina's head shots, which is a black-and-white photo with a listing of her acting credits on the back that she has to give to casting agents and producers to get acting parts.

"WOW!" Lucy said. "Your mum's an actress. She was on *Days of Our Lives*! We have that show here! Mum doesn't let me watch it."

"She was on *Days of Our Lives* for like a day," I mumbled. Angelina had two lines on one episode— "Help, Doctor, my boyfriend's been attacked!" and "Oh, God, he can't be dead!"—and then she screamed in glistening, white-toothed splendor. That was when Angelina had spent a month in Los Angeles for pilot season. She hadn't gotten any acting roles on new TV shows (the pilots), but she did get three commercials.

"And she was in *Home Alone Two*!" Lucy exclaimed.

"She was an extra," I groaned.

"She's beautiful!" Lucy said. "Her hair is so straight and long. The brown color is so shiny. That's probably why she's gotten all these hair commercials. She has a face like a doll's. You have the same shaped eyes as her. Angelina Waverly. What a great name." Lucy pronounced "great" like "graayate." She sounded exactly like Penny.

"Sounds better than Amy Finkelstein," I added. Angelina's birth name.

"She must be terribly rich from all those acting jobs. She must know loads of famous people."

"Hardly," I said. "She does okay. But mostly it's Bubbe's money. Bubbe pays for my private school. Bubbe paid for me to come here."

"What's she like, your mum?" Lucy was leaning into me. I could tell she was really curious about my other family.

I said, "EXCEPT for the fact that she is marrying Wheaties' dad, EXCEPT for the fact that she is having a baby without asking me first, EXCEPT for the fact that she thinks I am moving in with those people, Angelina is pretty cool, for a mom. She likes to go down to Greenwich Village to get coffee and yummy desserts, or to Soho to go shopping and to look at funky art. Our favorite place is the Cloisters, this really cool medieval museum uptown. She lets me pick her clothes for her auditions and her parties. We read together every night. We just finished this gothic romance called *Rebecca*. It was about this mousy lady who married this rich guy who she thought was still obsessed with his first wife. And the first wife's housekeeper at this ancient old mansion was really ticked off about the second wife and spooked the second wife practically to death. Angelina is hysterical to read with. She plays all the parts and makes these really funny faces and does great strange accents." I sighed. "Lately, though, she hasn't been around as much. She's been going away for lots of weekends with Wheaties' dad. And look what that's come to!"

Lucy said, "That's how Angus and I knew something serious was going on with our mum. When she extended her vacation to America by two extra weeks. We were staying with our Granny Nell. When Mum came back from America, she was like in this glowing other world. It was sickening almost! And she was engaged to your dad! Angus and I were sooooo mad."

"But you got Jack!" I protested.

"I know," Lucy said. "But we didn't know that then. We didn't know we were going to end up loving him. Mum had been married once before, about a year after our real dad died, and that was a disaster. She was miserable. Granny Nell was furious! The fights they had! For a while Mum didn't let us spend time with Granny Nell because Granny had been so mean about Mum getting married again."

"What happened?" I couldn't imagine not being allowed to see Bubbe anytime I wanted.

Lucy shrugged. "Dunno. The marriage never felt real, you know? It was like they were playing house, playing grown-up. His first wife was also dead. Mum explained after it was all over that maybe she and Patrick—that was our other stepdad—were just grieving. That they thought they were in love, but really they just needed somebody. Soon after Patrick moved out, Mum left for America to go 'figure things out,' as she said. That's when she and Granny Nell made up."

"Wow," I said. I had no idea the Steps had been through so much. I thought I had it bad, but they had lost a dad and a stepdad, and had a Jack-dad come into their lives without their invitation. Plus they had been moved around, it seemed like, every year.

"When your dad first came to Australia, I hated him," Lucy announced.

I jumped in my seat. "How could you hate Jack!"

"Well, I didn't know he was going to turn out to be, you know, Jack. I just thought he was some weird guy with a funny accent who probably wouldn't be around for long anyway, so why be nice to him? I tried hard to ignore him, but he wouldn't let me. He always wanted to take us places and read us books and play games with us. Mum was soooo happy. He talked about you all the time. You were the only thing that interested me about Jack at first. I thought it would be pretty cool to have a sister the same age as me in America, in New York. But every time he had you on the phone, you refused to talk to us. I should have known then that you'd be like that in person," Lucy said.

"Like what?"

"All snobby and picky. 'The Frosties don't taste right here.' 'You shouldn't wear that blouse with that skirt. It doesn't match.' 'Your television shows suck here.' 'I don't want to go to the museum, I want to go shopping.'"

You would think that I would have been mad that she was talking trash about me, but instead I laughed. Lucy did a perfect impression of my New York accent, and I had said all those exact words. I really had behaved badly.

"Sorry, sorta," I told Lucy. "But I was mad that you called him Dad. I thought he had forgotten all about me."

"You're crazy!" Lucy said. "He talks about you all the time. We talk about you all the time. It's like you've been this invisible member of the family for two years. You were always there, but we couldn't see you. He was so excited that you were finally coming to Australia."

Just then I felt really bad about running away. I hoped Jack and Penny wouldn't worry too much when they realized we were gone. Lucy must have felt kind of bad too, because she murmured, "We're really going to get into trouble for this."

"Big trouble," I said.

All of a sudden the people in the train car shouted out, "Five! Four! Three! Two! One! Happy New

Year!" They popped open champagne bottles and threw confetti into the air and kissed one another.

Don't ask me why, but suddenly I leaned over to Lucy and gave her a kiss on the cheek. "Happy New Year," I said. Tears came to her eyes, like she knew we were having a Moment. She hugged me.

I guess it was an okay way to start the New Year, by realizing my stepsister was pretty amazing. That she was my friend. My sister.

Chapter 16

All my life I have been waiting to experience what Brittany Carlson experiences with Brad Dufus the Third, what *Titanic* Rose experienced with Jack Dawson, what Lucy would like to experience with Bo, her E-mail love from Atlanta. I had no idea that the major crush factor would jump in live and in person right on New Year's Day. I guess that's the thing about love—it just kicks you in the face when you least expect it.

If I had known that Dream Boy was coming into my life that day, I might have hurried Lucy to our destination faster during those first couple of hours in Melbourne.

Lucy and I began our day in Melbourne by deciding to wait before heading to her grandmother's house. We knew we would be in big trouble once we got there, and we figured since we were already in trouble, we might as well have some fun first.

"My friends will be hanging out on the oval on New Year's Day," she promised. The oval was a game field in a park nearby her granny's.

We had changed out of our Kleenex-stuffed dresses and taken off the makeup from the night before in the train car bathroom. To mark our new solidarity, we traded outfits. Lucy wore my favorite summer outfit, a short stretch dress with a panoramic black-and-white picture of the Manhattan skyline for a pattern, with my black platform sandals. I wore Lucy's navy-and-white bike shorts, which, thank you, matched the striped Australian football T-shirt of Lucy's favorite Melbourne team, the Carlton Blues. We each kept our own hats, however. Lucy wore her straw hat, and I wore my "dreadful hat," as Lucy called it, the brown felt cowboy hat with the beads hanging down from the rim and the letter *A* on the front that I had bought at Paddington Market.

"That hat totally does not go with that outfit," Lucy said in the train station bathroom after we had changed, imitating my American accent.

I imitated her Australian accent, using the phrase everyone in Australia seemed to say at every opportunity. "Graayate!"

Lucy really knew her way around Melbourne, like I know Manhattan. Once we left the train station, we headed right for the tram, which was this neat old-fashioned bus-train combo that ran from cables hanging on the street.

As we put our fare into the tram machines Lucy's shoulders dropped a little in sadness. "The connies are all gone," she said. "They were the tram conductors who used to take everyone's fare. Now it's all done by machine. I've missed so many things since we moved to Sydney! I'm glad we ran away!"

The tram ride was not that long. Melbourne didn't feel like a big, vast city like Sydney, which was pumping with energy and activity. The streets in Melbourne seemed more polite, less hurried. There were a few skyscrapers in the middle of the city, where the train station was, but the rest of the city, at least the sections we had passed through on the tram, looked very quiet and somewhat industrial, like New Jersey without the noise.

We got off the tram on a street near the university (Lucy called it "uni") that was lined with Italian pastry and coffee shops. It was about nine in the morning, and I was starving. "Let's eat!" I said.

Lucy locked her arm in mine, grinning from ear to ear at the sight of her familiar old neighborhood. "The nice thing about having no parents around is we can eat anything we want for brekkie." She guided us into a milk bar and picked out a box of cookies and two Cokes.

"Cookies for breakfast?" I asked. But I wasn't complaining. I had discovered that Australia was not the place for a good old-fashioned American breakfast with pancakes, eggs, and home fries. In Australia brekkie feasts were not common like in America, and I had long ago given up on their Rice Bubbles (pathetic excuse for Rice Krispies), crumpets (English muffins), and pasty-looking bagels. Cookies I was more than willing to try. I added some Kinder Surprise chockies to our brekkie booty, figuring we could save the toys inside for Angus as a souvenir of our adventure.

"We are too sick," Lucy said. Between Lucy's piggy bank and the money Bubbe had given me, we could survive on junk food for a very, very long time.

We walked to the nearby park and sat down under a tree to eat. Lucy's cookies were rectangle-shaped chocolate sensations called Tim Tams. They were outrageously delicious—better even than Oreos! And no one loves Oreos more than me.

"This is the best breakfast I've ever had," I said. "What's for lunch?"

"Ice cream!" Lucy said.

After we had finished pigging out, we hung out under the tree, out of the blazing sun, for a good half hour, talking and playing mock drums against the tree trunk and doing handstands and cartwheels on the warm grass. We were wired with energy. Only once did I ask Lucy, "Do you think they're worried about us?" and she answered, "They probably haven't even figured out we're gone yet."

I don't think either of us believed that.

Chapter 17

Lucy looked at her watch. "It's almost ten thirty. The kids will probably be out by the oval about now," she said. I followed her through the park to the large, round, grassy field, which was ringed by a paved track for running or walking. A group of boys ranging from about age ten to fifteen were playing footy inside the oval. While we were sitting under the tree eating our junk food fest, Lucy had been trying to explain how the game worked. Footy seemed to me like a mixture of soccer, rugby, and American football. All the boys wore striped shirts like the one I had on, but they didn't wear helmets or padding like in American football, although their actual ball looked like an American football.

Lucy and I walked toward a group of girls our age who were watching the game from a small row of bleachers. "Lucy!" they cried out. They all started screaming and jumping up and down and hugging one another. I should have expected Lucy's friends would all be squealers.

When no one was surprised to see Lucy, I realized they had been expecting her, that she had been planning to run away all along. I realized she was angry at Penny not just for not letting her see her grandmother, but because Lucy wanted to visit with her own friends, her real friends.

"Great dress! Is that New York on the picture?" one girl called out. She had red hair just like Justine's, only this girl's hair was straight, and her face had freckles all over it. I knew from pictures Lucy had shown me on the train ride that the girl was Jenny, Lucy's BF.

"It's Annabel's dress," Lucy said to the group. She introduced them all to me one by one, but there was no way I could remember all their names. I called out hi and sat down. The girls all crowded around me, asking questions about America, but I could not concentrate. I was lovestruck by a vision in the center of the field.

"Who's he?" I asked of a boy who had just bounced into the air and made an amazing catch, or "mark," as they say in Australian footy. He had short brown hair that fell long in the front of his face, and his knee-high socks showed off great calf muscles. He was "foine," as we say at the Progress School, finer than any boy-band boy wonder I'd ever seen.

"That's Ben!" Jenny said. "Lucy's former step."

I looked at Lucy. "You didn't tell me you used to have other steps."

Lucy shrugged. "We weren't steps for long. Patrick and Mum were barely married a year."

"He's soooo cute," I mumbled, in a daze of wow. If he used to be Lucy's step, did that make him my step-step?

"Do you think?" Lucy asked, incredulous. She had obviously never taken any particular notice of Ben. She inspected him as he high-fived his teammates. "He has filled in a lot. Looks like he's gotten quite tall, actually. He used to be so skinny, even though he ate all the time. I think he just had a birthday. He would have just turned fourteen."

Fourteen! That meant he was a high school boy!

Lucy and Jenny paid little mind to the drool hanging out of my mouth. "Did you bring the stuff?" Jenny asked Lucy.

Lucy nodded and pulled a pack of cigarettes out of her backpack.

"Lucy!" I said. "I thought those were for pretend, for last night."

Lucy shook her head. "Jenny and I have been promising we would try cigarettes together next time we saw each other. I got them from a secret stash of smokes mum doesn't think I know about." She placed a cigarette in her mouth and handed one to Jenny, who did the same.

They looked so stupid. I couldn't believe this.

Jenny lit a match and tried to light Lucy's cig. Lucy took a big breath and then gagged as she tried to inhale. She coughed like mad. Jenny did the same when Lucy tried to light hers.

"You're doing it all wrong," I advised.

"YOU SMOKE?" the girls exclaimed.

"No, but my Bubbe does. Here, if you're going to do it, let me show you how to do it right." I crossed my legs on the bleacher and took my left shoe partially off, so it dangled from my foot. I tapped my fingers on the bleachers, extracted a cigarette from the pack, then lightly tapped the tobacco end on the bleacher surface to pack the tobacco. I put the cig in my mouth, ran my fingers through my hair, and lit a match. I took a very small puff and exhaled the smoke.

"You can't take really deep drags your first time," I said.

"Your grandmother told you that?" Lucy asked.

"Bubbe let me smoke after she caught me and Justine trying to sneak some of her cigs. She wanted me to see how disgusting it was. She was right! I was sick all night long. You will be too now." I made a face. "This is totally gross! You guys are dumb to smoke." I stubbed my cigarette out on the bleacher and coughed up some phlegm. Then I made my voice like Bubbe's and said, "I told you not to smoke, dahling!"

Some of the boys were heading our way. Lucy and

Jenny quickly put out their cigarettes. I grabbed the pack from Jenny's hand and took out the remaining cigarettes, broke them in half, and threw them into the trash can.

The boys were taking a break in the game. You could hear the nervous, excited energy from the girls on the bleachers as the boys approached.

Ben, love god, led the boys. "Hey, Lucy," he said.

"Hey." She shrugged. She was much smoother around her Melbourne friends than the Sydney kids.

Up close, Ben was not cover-boy handsome. He had big green eyes and an angular jaw, but his nose was a funny curvy shape, as if it had been broken several times in footy games, and his hair was wild, falling down the front of his face. He was sweaty and dirty from the game. I sighed.

Ben gestured to me. "Who's your friend, Luce?"

"That's Annabel. She's my new step. She's from America."

"Cool," Ben said. He inspected me head to toe. "Excellent hat," he said.

The girls all burst out laughing. I think my face turned the color of a tomato. I wondered if everybody could hear my heart pounding. No boy had ever had that effect on me before.

"Do you barrack for the Carlton Blues?" he asked. When I gave him what was probably a totally stupid, confused look, Ben pointed toward my striped navy shirt.

"Barrack?" I asked, looking around the oval for military living quarters.

"You know, who's your favorite team?" Ben said.

"Oh, you mean who do I root for?"

The boys and girls all laughed. Ben blushed. I was confused.

"That's a very naughty word here," Lucy whispered in my ear. "If you support a team, then that's the team you barrack for."

Oh.

I told Ben, "If that's Lucy's favorite footy team, I barrack for the Carlton Blues. But in America I barrack for the Baltimore Ravens." My favorite American football team.

"Are they good?" he asked.

"I don't know," I said. "But they have the best-looking uniforms."

All the girls broke out in giggles again. Ben looked disgusted with me for a second, then he laughed too. Everyone was listening to our conversation like we were famous lovestruck stars, like we were Romeo & Juliet, Jack & Rose. Like one day we'd be known as Ben & Annabel, not just Ben and Annabel.

"How old are you?" Ben asked.

"Almost thirteen," I answered. Thirteen in five months and five days!

"Your American accent is awesome," Ben said. "Where in the States are you from?"

"Manhattan, baby," I said, and swished my hair

over my shoulder. Did I hear myself properly? Man-hattan, *baby*?!?

"Cool," Ben said. He turned to Lucy. "You guys should come by later and say hi to my dad. He'll be glad to see you."

Ben checked me out again, grinned, and walked away just as abruptly as he'd stopped the game to come say hi. The pack of boys followed him and resumed the game.

All the girls on the bleachers were swooning. "He likes you!" they were whispering.

I was melting.

Chapter 18

Did I notice when noon rolled around and the sun was frying us? No. Lucy said we should leave for her grandma's house. Sadly, Ben didn't seem to notice when we left. His team was winning. I turned around once to see if Ben was watching us leave the park, but at that exact moment he missed his mark and stomped to another part of the field. Major bummer.

"I think I'm going to be sick," Lucy mumbled, clutching her stomach as we walked. "All the chockie, that cigarette, that sun. *Oy!*"

I guess it was lucky we had a place to go rest. I couldn't imagine how horrible it would be to be a real runaway, with no place to go if you were sick or tired, with no money for food.

Lucy's grandmother's house was only blocks away, on a street filled with rows of small, Snow White-looking houses. The house had gorgeous white iron latticework on the fence and porch trim. An older lady was sitting on a rocking chair as we walked up the sidewalk to the house. Her white hair was wrapped into a bun. She was big and round, not like Bubbe, who can never remind us enough that she may be in her late sixties, but she has not lost her "girlish figure." The lady had lovely rosy cheeks and big baby blues just like Lucy. She was sitting under a ceiling fan and talking on a portable phone.

"Here they come now," her voice crackled.

Lucy broke into tears and ran into her grandmother's arms. Her granny was crying too. Now I wanted to cry. Lucy's granny waved at me as she hugged Lucy. She handed me the phone.

"Hello?" I asked into the phone.

"ANNABEL!" Penny's voice sounded like a combination of rage and relief. "Thank God."

"Can I talk to Jack, Penny?" I said. Tears were welling in my eyes, and my voice cracked. There was a silence on the other end of the phone. Finally Penny came back to the phone and said, "Annabel, he's so furious he doesn't want to talk to either of you. I think you two have aged your father twenty years over the course of this day. *I* can barely speak to you. But don't you worry, we'll be talking about this for a long time soon enough. Please put Lucy's grandmother back on the phone."

"Sorry," I whispered, and I didn't mean sorta. I was crying for real now. I handed the phone back to Lucy's grandma and turned my back so Lucy wouldn't see me shaking. I couldn't believe I could make Jack so furious that he wouldn't even speak to me. I couldn't believe how bad I felt, like I had a ton of bricks in my stomach and butterflies twitching all over my nerves. All of a sudden I was so tired.

When she got off the phone, Lucy's grandma came over to me and patted my hair. She leaned down to talk into my ear and very softly said, "You must be Annabel. I'm Nell Crosswell. Lovely to meet you. Come inside, you girls must be exhausted." She kissed me on the head. I thought that gesture was so nice. I could see where Lucy got her kindness from. I really needed that kiss on the head.

I don't remember walking into Mrs. Crosswell's house or lying down to take a nap. So much had happened in the last twenty-four hours. Jack had killed my hopes that he would return home to America, Angelina had dropped her bomb, Lucy and I had run hundreds of miles away and become friends, Ben had crushed into my life with a vengeance. I needed sleep.

I woke up around five in the evening to find Lucy and Mrs. Crosswell sewing a quilt in the living room.

"I woke up an hour ago," Lucy said to me. "We're making a fish quilt for Angus. Grandma worked it out with Mum and Dad. We can stay another day and then go home."

Mrs. Crosswell pointed out, "Being allowed to stay is not a reward for your bad behavior. There are just no flights available for another day because of the holiday week. I'll take the two of you home myself. We're not trusting you two on a train ever again."

Lucy stifled a giggle. Mrs. Crosswell explained, "The train connie from Sydney went looking for you two when the train arrived in Melbourne. When he couldn't find you to reunite you with your sobered-up 'parents,' he found your ticket stubs and tracked down your reservation number. He called Penny."

Pretty clever, that train connie. I was dying to ask, *Since we've got an extra day until our impending punishment, could we go see Ben again now?* Lucy looked too cozy leaning on her gran's shoulder, though. I kept my mouth shut.

I looked around the room. It was quaint and pretty, with old-fashioned brocade upholstery and beautiful wood furniture and an ancient rocking chair. It smelled like an old person's house, but in the nicest way.

I walked over to the fireplace and looked at the pictures lining the mantelpiece.

"That's my real dad," Lucy said about the picture I picked up. He looked just like her: blond hair, rosy cheeks, intense baby blue eyes, proudly posing with his surfboard standing next to him. I couldn't believe how young Penny looked in the wedding picture with Lucy's dad. Her black hair was long, almost to her waist, like Morticia Addams, and her face looked young and alive, not subdued and a little tired, like she looks now.

When Lucy left the room to go to the bathroom, Mrs. Crosswell came over and wrapped her arms around me in a big hug! You'd think I would have been surprised, but I was learning that Lucy and her gran were very touchy-feely people. "I'm so glad you and Lucy have become sisters. She's needed a sister. Do you think your Bubbe, as you call her, would mind if I adopted you too? Since I lost my son, I can't get enough of my grandchildren. They're everything to me."

"I suppose there's always room for more grand-parents, Mrs. Crosswell," I said.

"Please call me Granny Nell," she said.

One thing Granny Nell had all over Bubbe was she could do some serious cooking. Angelina and I cook sometimes, but mostly Bubbe likes dinner to come from "our friend the deliveryman," as Bubbe says. Then Bubbe adds, "That's why we live in Manhattan, darling. We can have food from anywhere delivered anytime!" If only Bubbe had tasted Granny Nell's vegetarian lasagna and chocolate cake. Yum city!

When we finished eating, Granny Nell let me do the dishes. In fact, as part of her punishment to us (she promised more later from our parents), we had to spend the whole next day cleaning out her shed. *Oy.*

As Lucy and I dried the dishes Granny Nell said, "I'm so glad to have you two girls here with me." Then her tone changed. "But if you two EVER pull a

STUNT like that AGAIN, I will haul you into the police station myself! You have no IDEA what could have happened to you. The WORRY you caused your family. Rascals!"

That sweet lady meant it too. Lucy and I both looked down at the floor, ashamed.

Chapter 19

I tried to drag Lucy out of bed at six thirty the next morning. You know why, too. So we could hurry up and clean out the shed and then go visit Ben!

"Get up, Luce! Let's start cleaning!" I pulled the sheet off her.

She threw her arms over her eyes to block out the sunlight coming in from the windows. I'd thoughtfully opened the curtains and raised the blinds.

"GO BACK TO BED!" Lucy moaned. "I am."

Lucy grabbed the sheet back and rolled over onto her stomach with the sheet thrown over her head.

I ran into the kitchen. Granny Nell was making coffee.

"Can I get started on the shed now, Granny Nell?" I asked.

"What's your rush, lass?" she grumbled. She opened her newspaper.

Lucy and her grandmother were obviously not morning people. I had so much energy and excitement, I wanted to burst.

"Is it okay if I go for a run at the oval, Granny Nell?"

Granny Nell looked up from her paper. "You'll ask permission to go for a run two blocks away but not to run off unchaperoned on an overnight train from Sydney to Melbourne?" She shook her head and shooed me away with her hand. "Go, child. Be home in an hour. I'll be in better spirits to make you some brekkie once my coffee's had time to take effect."

I dressed in crinkly running pants and a matching jogging top and sprinted over to the oval. The sun had just risen, and the weather was balmy and warm, beautiful. Flowers were blooming along the sidelines of the oval. I sat down in the grass and smelled the sweet summer air. *Ben-Ben-Ben-Ben-Ben-Ben-Ben*, my mind hummed. He had probably been sitting on this grass less than twenty-four hours ago. Sweet grass!

I bent over my extended leg to do the stretching exercises Angelina and I do before we go running around the Central Park reservoir. As I was stretching my torso over my leg, I saw a shadow standing over me. I could not believe my luck.

"Hey, American girl," *THAT* voice said. "Where's your cool hat?" I had forsaken the "dreadful hat" for a New York Mets baseball cap.

I looked up and there he was standing. *Ben-Ben-Ben-Ben-Ben-Ben-Ben.*

"You made me miss my mark yesterday," he accused.

"What?" I asked.

"Yesterday. I had almost caught the ball, and then you and Lucy got up to leave and I lost track of the game for a second. We lost the game because of you."

How big was my grin? I couldn't tell you, because I didn't have a mirror, but it felt plastered across my face, and I desperately tried to squash it down so Ben would not see how pleased and flattered I was.

"What are you doing here so early?" I asked him, trying to think of safe conversation so I would not make a total idiot of myself. I stood up but lost my balance, instinctively grabbing for his arm as I started to fall down. He caught me and helped me up. My skin tingled from his touch. "I'm kinda klutzy," I blurted out.

"Klutzy?" Ben laughed. "What's that?"

"I stumble into things, fall down, trip, things like that. Klutzy. It's my grandma's word." *Shut up, Annabel,* I thought. *SHUT UP!*

"Well, klutzy," Ben said. "I come here every morning before school for a run. I come on holidays, too, because now it's become a habit. If I'm going to be a professional footy player one day, I have to train every chance I get."

I tested him. "Wouldn't you rather be playing on

your PlayStation instead of getting up so early in the morning to work out?"

Ben stared at me very seriously. "I'd much rather be playing footy or working out than be locked up inside playing on some dumb machine."

I had to turn around so he would not see me catch my breath. He joined me as I walked toward the oval.

"Do you work out?" he asked.

"I go running with my mom sometimes in Central Park," I said. "And I love to swim and rollerblade."

"Cool," Ben said. Without either of us inviting the other, we started jogging side by side along the pavement ringing the oval. "I've always wanted to visit New York. Seems like a fantastic city when you see it in movies or on the telly. Dad says maybe we'll go there for my sixteenth birthday. He's been saving for years for us to take an adventure somewhere."

"You should go!" I said. I turned around to run backward so I could face him. "It's the coolest city. You'd have to go to the Empire State Building because every tourist does that, but after you should go see the Chrysler Building, which is way cooler. It has this arch tower with art deco windows, and I think it's probably the most enchanted building in all of Manhattan. And you could go running around the reservoir in Central Park like Madonna does and go ice-skating at Rockefeller Center and of course you'd have to go to the Village to play pickup basketball, and then there's always lots of football or baseball games you could get in on in Riverside Park, maybe you could even teach the guys there how to play Australian footy."

I was talking a mile a minute, like I was Angelina. As I talked I gestured wildly with my hands I was so excited, and of course, running backward and flailing my arms about, not to mention my shoelace, which had come untied, I tripped and fell on the grass.

"Owww!" I cried out. *Could I just die right now?*

Ben stopped his jog and sat down on the grass next to me. He leaned in to touch my ankle, to see if it was okay, but then got really shy just before his hand reached my shoe. He pulled his hand back suddenly.

"You ok, klutzy?" he said instead. His smile and deep green eyes made me forget all about the sharp pain.

"Want to know a secret I haven't even told Lucy?" I said.

"Yeah!" he said quickly.

"My friends at home call me Whoops."

"Whoops?" Ben said.

"On account of I'm always falling and . . ." I hesitated, not sure whether I could trust him with this information. Then I decided I could, and I finished, "Because my full name is Annabel Whoopi Schubert. My middle name is Whoopi."

Here's how I knew I loved him. He didn't laugh.

"Cool," he said. I think that was his favorite word. From the way he pronounced the word, I bet he listened to a lot of hip-hop music.

I stood up and tried to start running again, but the pain in my ankle was too intense. "I think I'd better go home and put some ice on this foot," I said.

"I'll walk you," Ben said. I dare you to find one boy at the Progress School that chivalrous. I dare you further to find one with an Australian accent as sweet sounding. My ankle was hurting less already, but I hung on to his arm as I limped back to Granny Nell's anyway. Hanging on to arms is what Brittany Carlson does to Brad Dufus the Third, and even though she is the last of my idols, in the boyfriend department at least, I figured I could learn from her.

Ben's arm muscles were Australian Grade A *buff*!

"You'll be okay?" he asked me as we reached the gate to Granny Nell's. I nodded. I thought, *I'll be okay so long as I get to see you again!* I closed my eyes halfway in case he wanted to kiss me. He didn't.

"See ya, Whoops."

I opened my eyes back all the way to see Ben sprinting back toward the oval.

Chapter 20

Lucy came back into the shed we were cleaning with a pitcher of lemonade.

"Guess who's coming to dinner?" Lucy asked.

"Jenny?" I assumed.

"No, Jenny's coming to lunch. Patrick and Ben are coming to dinner. Patrick called and invited us over, but then Granny Nell asked them over instead. She loves to cook for people."

Ben was coming to dinner? I looked at my watch. That gave me only about seven hours to figure out what to wear.

"I thought your grandmother didn't get along with Ben's father," I said.

"Not so," Lucy said. "She just didn't like Mum marrying him barely a year after our dad died. She likes Patrick just fine. They live right down the street." I understood. Bubbe liked Jack just fine as my dad, but not as Angelina's "partner."

"Guess what else?" Lucy said. The shed was pretty dark, but I could tell she was smirking.

"What?"

"Well, Whoops, seems that our Ben has got a thing for . . . you!"

"He told you that?" That Ben had told Lucy my secret nickname didn't matter at all if he was crushing on me.

"Not exactly. He asked to talk to me after Patrick finished on the phone with Granny Nell. He said, 'Tell Whoops I said hi.'" Lucy paused. "Oh, don't look so surprised. Jack told us about your middle name when we watched *Sister Act*. You should feel lucky. Whoopi is a much cooler middle name than mine. Adelaide. Lucy Adelaide Crosswell. Dumb! Guess what else?" Lucy was having way too much fun with this.

"What?"

"Ben said you're the prettiest American girl he's ever seen besides Julia Roberts! He luuuvs your American accent."

"Ben's seen Julia Roberts?"

"No, silly!" Lucy said. "He lives in Melbourne! But if he had . . . then you'd be like, next prettiest."

Whoa! I thought my heart might jump out of my chest. I was twelve years old and facing massive punishment the next day, and still my life was this good.

It was hard to gloat about this new piece of information. Lucy was trying hard not to be sad. The shed we were cleaning was filled with old possessions of her dad's: old surfboards, woodworking equipment, microscopes, and tools. Lucy told me Penny had stored the stuff at Granny Nell's because she couldn't bear to look at her husband's things after he had died so suddenly, so young.

"Are you okay?" I asked. I poured her a lemonade.

"This whole week has been so intense," she said. "I want to cry seeing all his stuff. But it's like I'm out of tears. Remember how you said you were mad because Angus and I call Jack 'Dad'?" I nodded. Lucy continued, "Well, sometimes I wonder if my real dad is mad about it too."

"He's not," I told Lucy.

"How do you know?"

"Because if I can learn to deal with it, so could your real dad. Your dad would be glad that you and Jack found each other, like I am." If anybody had told me a week earlier that I would have admitted that, I would have wanted to spit in their face.

"Angus will probably end up being a marine biologist just like our real dad was," Lucy said. "Let's polish this equipment, and then we'll wrap the stuff and store it so we can keep it in good shape for when Angus grows up and wants it."

The last of Lucy's tears dried as she proceeded to work.

Chapter 21

Ben and his dad were really close. I thought that was really cool. Most of the boys I knew at school were embarrassed when their dad was around. But Ben, you could tell, really liked his dad. They were buds. They laughed the same laugh, smiled the same smile, talked the same topics.

"This casserole is graayate, Mrs. Crosswell!" Patrick said.

"Graayate!" Ben seconded. I am convinced "graayate" is the Australian national word, after any word cut off and ending in *ie*.

"They're all each other has," Granny Nell confided to me in the kitchen. Granny Nell didn't treat me like a guest. She let me help with the chopping, cooking, and serving. "Those two look after the other since Ben's mum passed and Patrick and Penny split up. That's the way it should be with fathers and sons!"

Then Granny Nell looked at me as I helped her pull a chocolate soufflé out of the oven. "Is that glitter on your eyelids?"

I grinned.

Granny Nell said, "Well, aren't you tarted up but lovely." I had borrowed back my panoramic New York picture dress and black platform sandals from Lucy. After Lucy and I had finished cleaning the shed, I had taken a shower and then put my hair in braids. I took the braids out right before Ben and his dad arrived, so that my hair fell down my back in blond waves. I added silver sparkle to my eyelids and a touch of pink lipstick to my lips. And Lucy, Jenny, and I had painted one another's toenails a funky purple color earlier that afternoon.

Patrick's and Ben's eyes widened very happily when we brought out the chocolate soufflé. It really was a special evening. Granny Nell had set up candles in the dining room, a lovely summer breeze was coming in through the lace curtains, and Duke Ellington jazz, which I knew because it was also one of Bubbe's favorites, was playing on the stereo.

Lucy and I knew it was our last night together before we had to return to Sydney and "be held accountable for our crimes," as Granny Nell said, and there was a mellow happiness between us. Like we knew our adventure was ending, but how glad we were to have had it. Ben's being there on our last evening of our adventure made the night more than perfect—it was bliss.

"Lucy," Patrick said. "Sydney's been good to you. You're growing into a lovely girl. You'll give your mother my best?" Lucy nodded shyly.

"How's my buddy Angus?" Ben asked. "Tell him thanks for the birthday card!" Lucy had told me that Ben was Angus's hero. Points for Angus.

"Mrs. Crosswell, this is the best chocolate soufflé I've ever had in my life." Granny Nell beamed at Patrick's compliment.

"Are you seeing anyone, dear?" Granny Nell asked Patrick.

"No time, really," Patrick said. He looked at Ben. "The boy keeps me pretty busy. We're training him for professional footy, you know. And he's going to work with me at some jobs this school holiday, right, son?" Ben's dad was a contractor who installed skylights, did electrical work, and generally made people's houses look and work amazingly, Lucy had told me. I could not name one boy at the Progress School who had a job with his dad.

Ben nodded eagerly, but his mouth was full. Another thing I liked about Ben was how unspoiled he was. He wasn't like those kids at the Progress School who can only talk about what computers their parents are going to get them, where their parents are taking them on vacation, what everyone could do for them. Ben was respectful and wanted to help his dad, instead of the other way around.

For some reason, seeing Patrick and Ben together

made me feel better about Harvey and Wheaties coming into my family. Having men around added an exciting energy to the dinner table.

Lucy said to her grandmother, "Ben's interested in learning how to surf over the school holidays. I was thinking maybe we could give him one of Dad's old surfboards? There would still be plenty left for me and Angus, Granny. What do you think?"

"If it's all right with you, it's all right with me. Those are your boards to give away, Lucy love."

I hadn't even realized the bait Lucy was throwing out until she said to me, "Annabel, why don't you go show Ben the surfboards in the shed while Granny and I make coffee?"

I love you Lucy, I thought.

Ben and I jumped up from the table and went to the shed outside. "Wow," Ben said when he saw how the shed glimmered in cleanliness and orderliness. "You and Luce really made this shed look great. I took some rakes out of here last winter to help Mrs. Crosswell clean up some leaves, and this shed was a mess!"

Now it was my turn to beam.

"You should come visit New York sometime," I said, searching for something, anything, to say.

"That would be fantastic," Ben said. *Fantastic.* Something only a megafine Australian guy would say.

The last specks of sunlight were shining into the shed as I showed Ben the surfboards. He stood up so close to me as we inspected the surfboards, and I could tell he was as nervous as I. He leaned in toward me, like maybe he wanted to touch my wavy-shiny hair, but then he pulled his hand back and touched one of the boards. "These surfboards are graayate," he admired. We both knew he didn't care about the surfboards at that particular moment.

I knew we didn't have much time before Lucy, Granny Nell, and Patrick came outside to join us. This was our moment, but Ben was too shy to make the most of it. So I took matters into my own hands.

I would never have done what I did next if Justine hadn't told me about the move from a sexy book she read. I reached for Ben's hand and placed it on my hip, then reached to put my arm on his shoulder. I smiled a closed-mouth smile so my braces would not twinkle in the twilight. Ben figured out the rest. He turned beet red, and if I hadn't known better, I would have sworn he was counting in his mind "One Mississippi, Two Mississippi, Three Mississippi . . ." before he leaned down. He finally moved his head down toward mine, and our lips touched in the best moment of my life that far.

I counted. The kiss lasted five heartbeats.

Chapter 22

I almost thought we had arrived at some parallel universe when we returned to Sydney the next morning. As Lucy, Granny Nell, and I walked out to the airport arrival area, who should be standing there waiting for us but: Penny and Jack, Angus holding Bubbe's hand, Beatrice in a Snugli on Angelina's chest, and Harvey and *Wheaties*? Excuse me?

"I told you there was a surprise waiting for you in Sydney," Granny Nell chuckled as we walked toward them. We had thought she meant a surprise garage to clean or that we would be—surprise!—grounded until the next millennium was halfway over.

Both Lucy and I looked at each other like, *Now what do we do?*

The moms came forward first. Penny grabbed Lucy toward her chest, and Angelina handed off Beatrice to Harvey and ran to me. "Oh, my baby," she said, squeezing me into the fiercest hug I'd ever experienced. She kissed the top of my head over and over.

"What are you doing here?" I asked, even though words were difficult. Angelina had my face nuzzled so hard to her chest it was difficult to breathe, much less speak. She smelled like Chanel perfume and baby powder.

Oh, no, I thought, *another airport scene.* I could just see future tourist billboard advertisements for Australia with pictures of me and the Steps and all our parents having weird reunions at the Sydney airport.

"After you hung up the phone on me, and I couldn't reach you by phone because you had unplugged it—you bad girl—I told Harvey we had to go to Australia right away to work this out. Bubbe said there was no way we were going to Australia without her, too. Harvey made hotel reservations, called the airline to cash in his million frequent flyer miles, and he had us on a plane to Sydney before I even had a chance to find out you had run away to Melbourne with Lucy. By the time we got here, you and Lucy were at Lucy's grandmother's. Your father might need to be hospitalized after the stress of these last few days. First you girls run away, then we show up unexpectedly. We're going to have a long talk this afternoon, young lady."

That "young lady" again. Since when had Jack and now Angelina, too, become so . . . so . . . parental?

Jack broke away from hugging Lucy and lifted me in his arms like I was still a baby. Tears were in his eyes. His big, tall body was heavy with relief and happiness.

"Anna-the-Belle," he murmured. And I'd thought Angelina's squeeze was tight.

"I'm so sorry, Jack," I said. "Please don't be furious with me." I tried to be cool, but the tears were streaming down my face and I was bawling like a baby.

"Kiddo," Jack said. *Uh-oh*, I thought. Nothing good ever comes of a conversation a parent starts with the word *kiddo*. "Maybe it's time you started calling me Dad."

I nodded into his neck and wished to stay in his arms forever.

Lucy and I were not allowed to go home right away. The first thing our parents did after releasing us from hugs and kisses was to sit us down. At the airport terminal, with a Sydney police officer they'd brought along!

The officer had a notebook filled with pictures of kids our age who had run away. Pictures of kids who were starving, who had been beaten, whose eyes begged for safety and warmth. Kids who had ended up homeless on the streets or lost forever, or worse, had been found dead. Lucy and I were shaking by the time the officer finished showing us the pictures.

"Do you understand the risks you two took?" he asked.

We both nodded. I think we were too shocked and horrified by the pictures to speak.

The officer said, "Maybe you think you were having fun and making a point to your parents at the same time, but what you did was stupid. Bloody stupid. You two don't know how lucky you were to make it to Lucy's grandmother's safely. Don't ever do anything like that again if you value your families or your life."

We both gulped. We understood. Big time.

Chapter 23

Angelina and I had the long talk, "young lady," in her hotel room.

I had never stayed in a fancy hotel before. The beds were gigantic, and the curtains looked like they belonged in a museum. Our suite had plush sofas and armchairs, too. Harvey is very rich. He owns a chain of mattress stores all over the tristate area. He's on television more than all of Angelina's shampoo, telephone, and panty hose commercials combined. "Hi, I'm Harvey Weideman. You can trust your good night's sleep to me." *Oy.*

Bubbe, Harvey, and Wheaties spent the afternoon lounging by the pool while Angelina and I talked. Bubbe must have been weighed down by ten pounds of bridal and wedding magazines.

"What is going on with you?" Angelina asked when we were finally alone together. We drank herbal tea from a formal silver tea set. "Talk to me," she said, and she did not sound like she was in a commercial.

I didn't have quite the words to answer. There was too much to say!

Angelina said, "I can't help you unless I know what's bothering you."

I started with, "You and Jack broke up, then he moved away, and I had steps and a half sister. Now you're getting married, and I'll have another step and another half sib coming. I'm sick of it!"

"What would you have us do?" Angelina asked. "Not find other partners? Not ever be in love again? Not share our love with anyone but you?"

I hadn't considered it from this angle. "Hmm," I said. I guessed now was not the time to tell Angelina about Ben and my first kiss.

"Annabel baby?"

"It's not that I don't want you to be happy," I said. "But it's so many people, so quickly. And I only just started to like Lucy and Angus, and now I have to live with Wheaties?"

"His name is Alan," Angelina pointed out. So that was his real name! Maybe everyone's called him Wheaties since nursery school because Alan sounds like a grown-up's name.

"Babies cry all the time!" I said. "Did you know that?" Beatrice was adorable, but try sleeping or reading or playing when she was hungry or tired!

Angelina laughed. "I remember. And I got a good reminder last night at dinner with Jack and Penny."

"That's another thing," I said. "I don't like it that you and Jack are still sore at each other. It makes me feel very strange if I want to talk to him about you, or to you about him. I don't like feeling I have to talk in secret to him on the phone so you won't hear us and feel bad all over again, or like I can't tell Jack about you because he gets all stressed hearing about you."

Angelina stroked my hair. "I know. Your father and I were so young when we had you. We haven't always handled things in the best way. Only now that we're thirtysomething senior citizens of the world are we starting to figure out what we want and who we want to be with. But your dad and I would never, ever want you to feel awkward because we weren't able to work things out between us. That's why we got together for dinner last night. To try to make peace. To become friends. For your sake, and for ours. It's a pretty terrible thing to stay angry at someone for so long."

"Really?" I asked. If Jack and Angelina could be friends, that would be a dream to me.

"We're going to try, baby. We're trying."

I smiled.

Angelina said, "Guess what else? Yesterday Bubbe took Alan and Angus on a ferry ride around Sydney Harbour while Harvey and I had dinner with Jack and Penny. I think Angus is Bubbe's new boyfriend. They've developed quite an attachment."

"She probably let him eat all the ice cream he wanted," I said.

"Probably," Angelina laughed.

"I like living at Bubbe's, Angelina," I said.

"Annabel, I'm your mother. I think we've been just a little too cool with each other. It would be my privilege, honor, and joy for you to call me Mom."

"Mom," I muttered. How weird did that feel tripping off my tongue? Weird and exotic and just fine with me. I tried the name out again. "*Mom*, I'm not ready to move."

"Bubbe, Harvey, and I talked about that on the plane ride over. Once we've found a place to buy, it will still be a few months before we could move in. So until then, we thought we could go slow, to give you time to become comfortable with this new arrangement. We thought you could spend weeknights at Bubbe's and weekends at Harvey's. And when we do move, we're planning to buy an apartment in the same neighborhood as Bubbe, so you'll never be far."

"What about Wheaties?" I said.

"Alan," Angelina-Mom reminded me.

"Alan," I said, and rolled my eyes. I wasn't being fresh. Wheaties sounded better.

"He'll stay with Harvey and me. His mom lives in California."

"He doesn't have a problem with that?"

"Not that he's told us. He's been reading the real estate listings for us, actually. He's pretty excited to move to a new apartment and have a baby brother or sister." Wheaties had adored Angelina since nursery school. When we were four, he used to run into her arms so he could sniff her hair. I guess I was glad for him to have a stepmom-to-be as nice as Angelina, er, Mom.

All of a sudden Angelina-Mom jumped up from the sofa and ran into the bathroom. "I'll be right back!" she called out.

When she returned, she said, "Morning sickness. This pregnancy has been more like twenty-four/seven sickness, though."

"Was I like that when you were pregnant with me, Mom?"

She took me in her arms and held me close. "You were perfect from the moment I found out I was pregnant. I love you, baby."

"I love you, too, Ange—Mom." I knew I was lucky to have her and Jack's safety and warmth.

Chapter 24

"How long are you grounded for?" Lucy asked when we arrived at the Steps' house in Balmain for dinner.

"I'm not grounded," I told Lucy. "It's worse. I get no allowance for six months, which means no shopping. I am banned from Bloomingdale's. But Harvey said in a couple of months, after the wedding, I could earn a couple bucks by helping him do inventory at one of his stores for a few hours on weekends. And no movies or TV for three months. What about you, Luce?"

"The weirdest thing," Lucy said. "I'm not grounded either. My punishment is that I have to make a new friend here in Sydney every week for the next two months and invite that person over to dinner or to a movie. And I have to spend five hours a week at Mum's aerobics studio sweeping, cleaning, and filing papers."

I gave Penny props for thinking up Lucy's punishment. The best way for Lucy not to want to run away ever again was for her to feel like she had friends in her new home. Penny and Granny Nell, I guess, had also had a long conversation about learning to get along better. And when Bubbe kissed Jack-Dad's cheek as she walked in the door, I knew they would be okay together.

In all, I thought my punishment very Ben-worthy. I vowed to spend the time I would have spent watching TV or going to the movies at the running track, so that the next time I saw Ben, he would be impressed with my amazing speed and all-over buffitude.

Also, if Ben could spend his holidays working with Patrick, then I supposed I could learn to deal with working with my stepdad for a few hours every week. At least I could say this about Harvey: He was a great dresser. He wore nice tailored Italian suits and beautiful silk ties. Plus, Harvey was one man you'd never see wearing Birkenstocks. Unlike his son, Wheaties.

"Your-almost stepbrother is such a dag," Lucy whispered in my ear. "Dag" is this Australian expression for a person who is nerdy, but in the best, most endearing kind of way.

"Way dag," I said.

Wheaties walked over to us. The top of his head barely reached our noses, his hair was slicked back with mousse, and he was pale as Wonder bread.

Wheaties said to Lucy, "I saw your smiley-face

curtains. Are you a fan of music from the seventies, like the Partridge Family?"

"Wheaties," I said. "In Australia you're not a fan, you're a supporter."

Wheaties repeated to Lucy, "Are you a seventies music fan?" Wheaties never lets me get under his skin.

Lucy flashed her multicolored-braces Lucy-love grin. She nodded enthusiastically, even though there is no Nick at Nite in Australia—and no way Lucy knew who the Partridge Family were.

"You like seventies music, Wheaties?" I asked. Aside from how weird it was to have this little slice of the Progress School on the Upper West Side sharing Balmain, Sydney, Australia, and the Steps with me (that was my other life), I could not believe Wheaties would like a group that wasn't singing obscure folk songs or picking instruments with names like Dobro or mandolin.

"I love the Partridge Family," Wheaties said in this voice like he was a game-show announcer. "They're true pop music wonders. Like the Beatles, like Madonna, they have a certain quality . . ."

I tuned him out. Lucy hung on his every word. She looked at him like she was getting a case of the Bens.

Penny came over to me and gently touched my shoulder. She didn't smother me in a hug or try to plant any unwelcome, phony stepkisses. She said, "I need your help outside." I walked with her to the backyard, where a big picnic table was sitting on the grass. "You'll see the plates and silverware waiting for you on the bench seat. If you'll put down the table-cloth and then set the table, Granny Nell and I should have dinner ready in about fifteen minutes."

I smiled at Penny. Guests were never asked to set the table. "Those black riding boots you wear are really cool looking, Penny," I said. The ends of her lips turned slightly upwards. Like her daughter, she knew when we were having a Moment.

"Thank you, Anna-the-Belle," she said, and walked back to the kitchen.

I stayed by my dad's side throughout the whole dinner. I didn't even want him to hold Beatrice. I wanted him all to myself. I held Beatrice instead, and miracle of all miracles, she managed to make it through most of the meal without crying or spitting up on me. Maybe she knew it was my last night in Australia, and she wanted to be extra good so I would come back and kiss the baby hair on her forehead over and over and rub my nose along her soft baby skin again.

On my other side sat Angus, who sat next to Bubbe, who sat next to Granny Nell. On the other side of the bench were Penny, Lucy, Wheaties, Angelina, and Harvey. It was like we were one big family. It was graayate.

"You're pretty good holding babies, Annabel," Harvey said. He was very talkative, I guess because he gets so much practice talking on television and talking to customers, convincing them to buy premium mattresses with expensive bed frames. He might also have been especially talkative because he hated the food—Granny Nell had made a delish vegan rice-tofu-veggies combo (in support of Wheaties) with the wok Jack and Penny had given her for Christmas. I knew Harvey and Angelina would order steaks in their fancy hotel room as soon as they returned, but I didn't care. What was important to me was that they had come. Harvey added, "Do you have any interest in designing some patterns for baby crib linens?" Did I! He added to Penny, "This Australian wine is outstanding!" Step-step talk.

Lucy said, "Mum, Patrick says hello. He and Ben came over for dinner." Something about the way Lucy said "Ben," and how Lucy and I started giggling after that beautiful word, made Angelina's eyes dart suddenly between me and Lucy.

"Who's Ben?" Angelina asked Lucy.

"Ask Whoops over there," Lucy giggled again.

I was drinking from a Coke bottle, and just looking at her made me laugh, which made me snarf. I handed the baby to Jack so I could wipe the Coke dribbling out of my nose. Wheaties laughed the hardest at my snarfing.

"Dis-gus-ting!" he said. "I can't wait to tell Brittany Carlson that Whoops Schubert snarfed her Coke at the dinner table in Australia."

"Ha-ha, Wheaties," I said. Angelina, a.k.a. Mom, shot me a look. "Alan," I said.

Wheaties said, "Nobody calls me Alan, Whoops." I shot Angelina-Mom a look like, *see*?

Angus asked, "Why do they call you Whoops?" I didn't need Angus to be added to the list of people calling me Whoops. Now was the perfect time to make Angus forget all about that nickname. I took the souvenirs out of my pant pocket. "Here, Angus," I said. "These are Kinder Surprise toys I saved for you."

"You ate Kinder Surprises without me?" he asked, "Whoops" forgotten.

Bubbe to the rescue. "You can't trust twelve-year-old girls with chocolate, Angus. I happen to have two chockies in my pocketbook. I'll eat some with you." Angus was in love.

Granny Nell informed the group, "Ben and Annabel took quite a fancy to each other, I'd say. I believe he's the prime suspect for those flowers left on the porch this morning with no note." Granny Nell chuckled.

From across the table Angelina, my mom, mouthed the word "Later" to me, meaning I had plenty of time on the plane ride home to New York the next day to cough up the scoopage.

Jack passed Beatrice over to Penny and said to me, "Let's go inside, just us two."

We both went inside, and I said, "What?" thinking maybe I was in trouble again.

"There's no what," Jack, my dad, said. "I just wanted to have a few minutes alone with you." His face looked so sad. I sat down on the couch and cuddled my head against his shoulder. He put his arm around the back of my neck and stroked my hair. "Seems like you just got here, and now you're leaving. You realize how much I miss you, don't you?"

I nodded. I knew, but it felt good to hear him say it.

"Your mom and I talked. We agree you should spend more time here. And Penny and I would like Australia to be just as much of your home as Manhattan is. How does spending the month of July here sound, as well as three weeks over the Christmas holidays? Your mom and I have agreed that you could miss a few extra days of school over the Christmas holidays in order to spend time with this family. Lucy and Angus will be in school part of the time you'd be here in July, but that will give you and me time to spend together, just us two. And next Christmas maybe we could go up to the beaches in Queensland—"

"Beatrice will be walking by then!" I said. She was already almost ready to crawl. She would sit on her hands and knees and rock her body back and forth while Angus encouraged, "Go, Beatrice! Crawl!"

Dad added, "She'll be talking up a storm by then too. Soon after you started walking, you started talking so much your mother and I wondered if you were making up for the time when you were a small baby and didn't know any words!" He paused, then looked down into my face. "And what's this about Ben? I don't know if I'm ready for my baby to have a boy sending her flowers."

"I'm not a baby, Dad," I said. Then, in a very low voice, I added, "I like the Steps."

"I'm glad," he said, "because we're going to be a family for a very, very long time."

When I left Manhattan for Australia, I had never imagined that I would return home a little more than a week later with not one, but two, more families. I hadn't liked the idea of having so many families, but the Steps were not my choice. What was my choice was whether or not I would make the best of my new family situations.

I breathed in the hot summer air coming in through the window. The next day I would return to winter. I would return with warm dreams of Australia, of an almost-boyfriend and an almost-BF step.

"Graayate, Dad!" I said. The sweetest words.

Epilogue

E-mail to: Annabel Schubert
From: Lucy Crosswell

Hey, Whoops! Sorry I couldn't write you back yesterday. I was at a slumber party at my new friend Jessica's house. You would like her a lot. She knows everything about fashion designers, like you do, and she wears hats even more dreadful than yours! I was so excited to hear about your new room in your new apartment. Wow, a skylight! Tell Harvey thanks for putting an extra bed in the room for me! And tell your mum I loved the acting books she sent, thank you sooooo much! I can't wait to come visit you in NEW YORK in June. I can't believe you let Harvey and Angelina give you my airplane ticket as your birthday present, since I get to be the one who gets to take the fabu trip, but GRAAAY-ATE! Angus is very jealous, but I explained to him that he isn't old enough to take a trip like that on his own.

Did I tell you? I talked to Jenny on the phone, and she said that Ben put the picture you sent him in his locker, and he pasted it to the door with a sticker of an American flag. <<Smooching sounds.>> Mum just put up a framed picture of you in the living room—it's you walking around in a swarm of people at Paddington Market, trying on that cowboy hat with the "A" and smiling this marvie smile. She also snapped one of the two of us holding Dad's hands and you sticking your tongue out at me behind his back and me not even noticing. We laughed so hard when we saw the picture! Mum is sending copies of the pics to your mum as a wedding present. Are you ready for the new baby in August? You HAVE to play me the tape of Harvey's new commercial with Angelina as the pregnant lady looking for a baby crib! You will not believe it, Beatrice is walking all over the place. We had to totally reorganize the house so she would not bump into things and grab things she shouldn't have. She has lots more hair, and Dad and I think she looks just like Mum, except she has the same exact nose as YOU. Oh, well, I have to get off now because Angus keeps pestering me to use the computer (he says hi and when will your gran send him more chockie?). Tell Wheaties that Mum found her old record of some Partridge Family tune called "C'mon Get Happy," and now that's Angus's fave song. Angus keeps playing the record over and over, so now Dad and I have renamed the song "C'mon Get Annoyed."

Tell Wheaties a super-extra-special hi from ME!

Luv, Luce